The Duke's Library

Laura Cabrerizo

The Duke's Library

Published through Amazon

First edition, print on demand

This is a work of fiction. Names, characters, businesses, places, events, locales, and incidents are either the products of the author's imagination or used in a fictitious manner. Any resemblance to actual persons, living or dead, or actual events is purely coincidental.

The Duke's

Library

Laura Cabrerizo

Table of Contents

This book is dedicated to my Grandmother Marie. She taught me everything I know about card games.

I love you and please skip the end of chapter 15!

Chapter 1

Bitter cold air swirled through the open doors of the ballroom. People, dressed in the finery of their stations, mingled far away from the arctic currents, while debutantes and their suitors swirled around the dance floor in lively cotillion. Gems glittered in the light cast by hundreds of candles as the highest echelons of the ton preened and postured for one another.

Ria ran gloved hands over her arms, trying to return warmth to them. She paid no mind to the fact that her gloves were fraying and her dress was from the Season before last, a leftover from her cousin's wife, Lydia. Trying to keep her chin up, she observed the young girls starting a new Season with hope and laughter brimming in their eyes and faces. They ignored the older women who pointed with fans and gossiped to one another. Her failure was always a favorite topic of conversation though time lessened her shame as new scandals unfolded.

She glanced over at the couch where the spinsters sat in silence while watching the proceedings. Though not one of them, she wondered if she would fall into the malaise that overcame this corner of the room when she joined them. Ria grimaced, not wanting to look into that sad but near future.

In just a few more moments, as soon as Lydia went to freshen herself, she could make her escape. She hated the balls and events that Season forced upon her, but her grandfather made her come. He still held hopes she would find a husband to make her happy. Well into her mid twenties, she knew it was a lost cause. She would rather stay home and read.

They were guests in the house of the Duke of Northumberland who was hosting a private ball before the official open the Season. The Duke's grandfather and hers had been fast friends, and so they had been extended an invitation to the event as a courtesy. Lydia and her younger sister, Lacy, had gossiped about the Duke most of the way to the ball. From what she overheard, the Duke was an intelligent and wealthy man who held titles and land throughout Europe and the Americas.

Considered the catch of the ton, mothers coveted invitations to the Duke's events, though he thus far eluded capture. Ria didn't concern herself with such pastimes. The pièce de résistance, in her mind, was the grand library in this mansion. When touring the residence earlier, she spotted a back entrance into the room and intended to visit as soon as she could slip away.

Out of the corner of her eye, Ria saw Lydia leave with a group of her friends. Delaying for a moment to make sure they didn't return, she backed towards the open doors to the veranda with slow and steady steps so she wouldn't draw attention to herself.

She noticed the stairs leading down into the gardens and a path around the house earlier in the evening. Rushing along the path, she kept to the shadows to conceal her presence. Her heart beat faster from the exhilaration of her clandestine adventure, at least in her mind it was.

Rounding the corner, she reached another set of doors off of a small patio. Peering around the corner to see if the coast was clear, she tried the knob, praying the doors would open. They offered no resistance to her hesitant tugging, and she slipped into the empty room, closing the doors behind her and leaning her back against them.

As she looked up, her mouth fell open with a gasp. The room was amazing! Books lined shelves two stories high with a winding staircase in one corner leading to the upper level encased in a twining wrought iron railing. Tucked between the bookshelves, windowed alcoves ran along the walls with padded seats for comfort and covered oil lamps for light.

The entire room was a rich rosewood color which helped to highlight the books it contained, their various sized spines and colors beckoning her touch. A fire crackled in the hearth surrounded by deep armchairs and a small couch in brown leather. Expensive Persian rugs lined the hardwood floors in counterpoint to a bright mural on the domed ceiling. A large desk sat in the corner near the fireplace with its back to the windows, littered with papers as if someone spent many hours a day working there.

Ria walked to the closest shelf and browsed through the books. She cringed at the disarray she saw. Science books mixed with history books which had books of poetry and art jumbled between them. Anthologies were mixed with biographies, and there were even a few books of fairy tales tossed in with disarray. Delighted to see more books and small pieces of artwork in one place than she had seen before, she worked hard to school her emotions amongst the towering shelves.

Picking up a book on science, Ria walked to the couch in front of the fire and reclined back, curling her legs under her and settling herself. She breathed in the musk of leather, parchment, and ink. Her muscles relaxed as she exhaled and set in for a good read.

Ria lost track of time. Buried in spellbinding descriptions of animalistic evolution she startled when she heard the door on the other side of the room open. Four men walked through, talking amongst themselves as they entered. Jumping from the couch, her heart pounding at their unexpected entrance, she searched for an escape. She cringed when she realized the only other exit was the doors she had come through.

The men stopped talking when they saw her, and the leader of the small group frowned. He kept a rigid posture; his hands clenched at his sides. He was tall and slender, his black waistcoat and breeches cut to accent his trim waistline and long legs. His black, piercing eyes narrowed as he pursed his lips, accenting his strong jawline and high cheekbones. His dark hair was short and parted to one side, curling against tanned skin that hinted at a Spanish heritage.

"This room is unavailable to guests," he said, his voice a deep baritone.

Ria grasped the book she was holding to her chest with a white-knuckled grip. The servants, earlier in the day, had barricaded the hallway doors with rope to indicate the rooms unavailability. It was the reason she found a back-way in. His gaze was disconcerting, and she was becoming more nervous by the second. She refused to look him in the eye and instead studied his shoes as she sidled towards the door she had entered through.

"I'm sorry," she murmured, "It's just…" Ria looked around the room once more, her face filled with wonder. "Your library is amazing. I've read all the books in ours at home and I never imagined there could be so many in one place. I couldn't help but see it."

With the last, stumbling words leaving her mouth, she placed the book she was holding on a small table and made a break for the doors to the patio.

Running through them, she slammed the door closed behind her glancing back up at the men. The leader was watching after her but speaking to the man next to him. Ria ran back towards the doors to the ballroom, hoping she wouldn't be in too much trouble with her cousin for being away so long.

As she entered the ballroom, she released a relieved breath when she realized that no one had missed her. No one ever missed her. She didn't know why she was so worried. She stood in an empty corner of the ballroom, enfolded in shadows, daydreaming about the room she had just been in while ignoring the surrounding people. The library had been an amazing sight, one she wouldn't soon forget.

Andres, Duke of Northumberland, watched the woman run out the door and turned to his brother. "Who was she?"

"Miss Victoria Sutton, if I'm not mistaken. She is the granddaughter of the Earl of Amberley and the niece of Baron Weston," Vincente, Vince to his close family and friends, replied.

Andres picked up the book she had been reading, turning it over in his hands. It was one of the newer books on the theory of evolution a colleague recommended to him. The book wasn't a light read by any means.

He tapped the book against his palm, considering her. She was a small thing, standing only as high as his chest, with ringlets the color of honey framing her face. She'd been wearing a pale blue dress, old and fraying around the edges of the bodice and sleeves, that matched well with her skin tone. It didn't fit her curves well, being too light in places and loose in others, and looked like it wasn't made with her figure in mind.

"What do you know about her?" He walked to the desk, still carrying the book, checking for any disturbance among the papers and items stacked on top of it.

"She's nearly a spinster; her first Season was around ten or so years ago. She stays with Amberley while in London. I have heard nothing else about her. She has no scandals attached to her," Vince replied, taking a seat across from the desk in a deep armchair with the other two men following suit.

Andres sat down behind the desk, placing the book to the side, to discuss the current affairs with his men. While they talked, his mind kept wandering back to the book on the corner of his desk and the woman who had held it. Ending the meeting, he dismissed his friends back to the party. He picked up the book and went to find Miss Sutton.

Ria was swaying to the music, wishing she could dance. It had been a long time since anyone had asked her. Her dance card dried up long ago. She was so entranced it took a moment for her to realize someone was next to her and glanced to the side to find the Duke standing there. He watched the dancers, paying her no mind, as if he hadn't even registered her presence.

Frozen in place, her hands at her side, she clutched her fan as if holding on to it for dear life. She didn't understand why the man would seek her out, except to reprimand her for going where she shouldn't. If Lydia saw her, she would never hear the end of it.

"I've decided to let you borrow this," he said, pressing something into her hand without looking at her. "If you bring it back in good condition, I will consider letting you borrow another one."

She realized it was a book, and she gave a half nod, not saying a word while hiding the tome in her wrist bag. The Duke walked away without a backward glance, the entire exchange taking mere moments. If someone saw, she would say he had stopped to observe the gathering. He hadn't said a word to her. Knowing he would also deny any association with her, she felt relieved and yet giddy with anticipation. She couldn't wait to get home and finish the book she now carried in her possession.

Noticing Lydia signaling to her, Ria walked around the ballroom towards her. She avoided the dancers and groups of men surrounding several young women. These were the belles of the Season, the top choices of the Marriage Mart.

"Look at Lacey! I'd estimate her first ball was a success," Lydia said as Ria stopped next to her. Ria glanced over her shoulder at the girl. Lydia was acting as a chaperone for her younger sister whom the gentlemen surrounded, looking for her favor. Playing with a loose strand of pale, blonde hair from the mass atop her head, Lacey smiled at the men, batting her eyes at one or two in particular.

"I expect we will have several callers tomorrow morning," stated Lydia.

Ria gave a non-committal noise. Lacey may be beautiful, but she was a terror to deal with. Her temper tantrums had become legendary in their home with the servants trying to avoid her at all costs. She felt sorry for the man that ended up married to her.

"I'm quite relieved. I remember your coming out, Victoria, and what a disaster it was," Lydia snickered, "Although, I wouldn't expect anything less from Lacey." Ria cringed at the use of her full name but said nothing.

"Attend her while I go find Christian so we can leave, I'd like to go before there is a line."

Watching Lydia walk away in search of her husband, Ria thought back to her own coming out. She had always been short and curvy instead of the tall, statuesque proportions which men seemed to favor. The dress she had for her coming out was yet another cast off from an older cousin. The seamstress altered the dress for her size but it had never fit right. Now that she thought about it, that summed up her experience in the ton, altered but never fit.

Her father, though a Lord by courtesy, was not the most industrious of his siblings and hadn't been able to afford a new wardrobe for her every year. Still, there were one or two men who showed interest in a marriage contract with her, until her brother's carelessness ruined her prospects.

Her brother's actions along with her introverted nature made it difficult to draw positive attention to herself. By the end of her first Season, she'd made no impression on any of the gentlemen. She wasn't even sure if they had remembered her, several of the ton asking her if she was new the next Season. It had been tempting to say yes. However, she didn't want to get caught in a lie, anything being fair game for the wagging tongues.

Chapter 2

R ia sat at the far end of the drawing room the next afternoon. She held the borrowed book opened in her lap while she tried to ignore Lydia. The feat was almost impossible.

Lydia was crooning over her little sister, telling her how wonderful and beautiful she was, stroking her ego to even greater proportions. Lacey had spent the previous night's ride home extolling the virtues of each man she had danced with and who might call today.

Ria wanted to gag but kept her thoughts to herself. Required to attend the two women, it was her duty to entertain any young gentlemen that may call whom Lacey wasn't interested in. Not that Lacey's suitors stayed long once she turned them away.

"Put that book down," Lydia hissed at her, causing her to jump. She sighed, closing the book, and placed it on an end table. "Where did you get it from, anyhow?"

"The library, of course," she gave her a blank stare. Lydia squinted at her for a moment, but it seemed luck was with her as a servant entered to announce their first caller.

The Marquess of Kentwood came with his younger sister, Lady Abigale, who was a particular friend of Lacey's. The younger girls gossiped together with their heads bent while Lord Kentwood spoke quietly with Lydia. He had a reputation for being a consummate womanizer and Ria suspected, from the way Lydia was looking at him, she was his current lover.

Ria wondered if Christian was aware and, if he was, even cared that is wife had affairs with other men. She knew her cousin and Lydia had a marriage of convenience, and there was little love lost between the two. Most of the time it seemed they couldn't stand being in one another's company.

Christian and Lydia's fathers had been good friends and business partners. When they had gone into a mining venture together, they made a marriage arrangement between their two children in hopes they would keep the business going when they retired.

Christian and Lydia had never gotten on well as children. Forced to spend summers together, Christian would hide in the great outdoors as often as possible while Lydia refused to soil herself by leaving the house.

Kentwood leaned closer to Lydia, whispering in her ear and making her blush. During Lydia's first season she caught Kentwood's eye and had, for a while, believed he would offer a marriage proposal that would free her from her parents' plans. It seemed he wasn't the marrying kind though he had no issues taking the benefits of a union without the commitment.

Through much perseverance, their family had been able to avoid scandal and keep Lydia's name out of the gossip circles. She never appreciated the efforts or the fact that Christian was still willing to marry her, not that he had much choice.

After the marriage contract was arranged, but before the wedding took place, both of Christian's parents fell ill with the flu. Neither of them were able to overcome the sickness. In the wake of their passing, Christian had appealed to their grandfather to break the engagement, but he had refused, saying it was what his parents had wanted. Ria knew it was one of her grandfather's greatest regrets in life, though he wouldn't admit it to anyone.

"And you will bring Abigale home tonight?" Kentwood asked Lydia as he turned to leave, breaking Ria out of her musings.

"Of course, My Lord," Lydia replied, giving him a smile Ria was sure Christian wouldn't approve of.

Kentwood's eyes flicked to Ria, his gaze slowly raking over her, and said to Lydia, "You should bring her with you sometime, it would be interesting."

"I will consider it," Lydia replied, her voice tight and eyes filled with anger directed at Ria. Kentwood walked out the parlor doors as Ria plotted her escape from the scathing insults she knew Lydia would throw at her. Luck seemed to be with her as new guests arrived before Lydia could make any comments.

 Soon the drawing room filled with people come to talk about the previous evening.

There were several first sons and wealthy merchants looking for a noble wife which made Lydia happy. Lacey and her friend flitted around the room, speaking to this person or that while a constant flow of guests arrived and left. Ria stayed in the corner, watching the proceedings but not taking part. No one noticed her.

Thankfully, visiting hours were drawing to a close as the visitors made their way to Hyde Park to posture and parade. She wondered, as she slipped out the door and up to her room while the mother of a boy interested in

Lacey occupied Lydia, if two days was long enough before returning the book and getting another. She was close to finishing the tome she'd borrowed, and the next evening, when her family left for the park, would be the perfect time to sneak away.

The next evening, at four o'clock sharp, her family left for their evening stroll in the park. They had taken what seemed like hours to get ready to leave the house. Ria, dressed in a serviceable walking gown, pulled her cloak tighter around her to ward off the chill of the afternoon as she made her way to the Duke's residence. After a half hour of brisk walking, she reached her destination. She considered using the servants' entrance but decided against it and walked to the front. A well-dressed butler opened the door, giving her worn out attire a disdainful glance. She was used to such treatment and tried not to take it to heart.

"May I help you?" his voice dripped with contempt.

"His Grace allowed me to borrow a book. He said if I returned it in good condition, he would let me borrow another."

He considered her for a moment and then opened the door wider to allow her entry. Taking her cloak, he told her, "His Grace is away for a fortnight, he left this morning. He mentioned that a woman might stop by to use the library. This way." Ria didn't realize she had been holding her breath, but when the butler opened the door for her, she released it with a soft sigh.

He led her through the entryway and down a long hallway towards the library. As they passed a maid creating a large arrangement of flowers on a table in the middle of the hall, Ria stopped to admire her handiwork.

"This arrangement is lovely," she said, smiling at the young girl. She bobbed a curtsey and smiled back. The butler watched, his face softening before continuing down the hall.

He stopped in front of the doors which were no longer roped off and opened them for her. Ria walked into the room, taking a deep breath of leather and parchment, her shoulders relaxing. She walked to the shelf she had taken the book from the other night and replaced it amongst its fellows. Running her finger along the spines of the books, she meandered around the room, looking for her next choice. The butler watched her with interest.

"Do you find anything that catches your eye?" he asked her.

Ria smiled as she looked around, "I feel like a child let loose in a candy shop, I have no idea what to try next, and every one of them looks delightful."

She pulled a book of poems from the shelf and looked over the cover. *Songs of Innocence and of Experience* by William Blake, it looked interesting, so she kept a hold of it while she looked through the others. She found several other books, but she was finally able to pare it down to two: the original book she had found, and a romance that looked like a fun read.

The butler cleared his throat, and Ria looked up at him startled. She had forgotten that he was standing there in her eagerness to look through the shelves. "Perhaps, if you cannot decide, you should take them both."

"Do you think it will be all right?" she asked, looking between him and the two books in her hands.

"I believe so," he replied, opening the door for her. She smiled at him, clutching both books in front of her, and walked out of the library.

"Thank you, I appreciate your kindness," she said as he wrapped her cloak around her to leave.

"The more you borrow at once, the less I have to deal with you," he grumped but winked at her as he let her out the door. She laughed and started on her way home, hoping to be back before her family left the park. She visited three more times over the next two weeks to borrow books, hoping to read as many as possible before the Duke returned.

Ria stood in front of the door to the Duke's townhouse with trepidation. According to the butler, His Grace should have arrived home the day before. She didn't know if he would still be of a mind to let her use the library. Slowly she walked up to the front doors and rang the bell, clutching the previous books she had borrowed in front of her.

The butler greeted her with a smile, having reevaluated his previous opinions of her over the last few weeks, and took her cloak. As he led her down the hall, her anxiety grew with every step. What-ifs and scenarios played through her head as the butler knocked on the door. A male voice called for them to enter and the butler opened the door for her, giving her a slight push through the portal when she hesitated.

The Duke sat behind his desk but paused with whatever he was writing to look up at her. He smiled and stood, walking around the desk.

"Good afternoon, Your Grace," she said, bobbing an awkward curtsy and not quite meeting his eye.

"Good afternoon to you, Miss Victoria," her eyes flew up in surprise when he called her by name, she hadn't known he knew it. "The servants have told me much about your visits." His voice was low and soothing, the tone one would use when talking to a frightened animal. "Come show me what you are returning today. I collect books from around the known world, but, sadly, I don't have the time to read most of them."

She looked down at the top book she was returning then walked towards him with hesitation. "This one expounds on the different species and habits of animals found in Africa."

"Which ones are your favorite?" he asked, looking at her face and tilting his head.

She grinned, "The lions I think. I watch our little house cat as he stalks the birds through the window and can't help but imagine him being a four-hundred-pound killer."

He laughed, "And the other book?"

"It's about the people and societies of India."

"I believe there is also a book about the animals of India," he said, looking around the large room.

"Would you know where?"

"No," he said grimacing, "I tend to just place them wherever they fit when I bring them home." She raised her eyebrows, looking at him. He gazed at her for a moment and said, "I have a proposal for you."

"Oh?" she asked with nervous anticipation.

"Come two or three days a week, arrange the books in the library, and I will let you continue to borrow any of the books you'd like."

A smile spread across her face, causing it to light up with joy, "I would love to sort the library!"

"Good," he laughed, "Then you can start now."

He nodded to her and walked back to his desk while she considered where to start first. Taking a deep breath, she walked over to the far wall and considered the bookcase in front of her. It was one reaching from floor to ceiling, and she would need to find a ladder. She pulled books off the lower shelves and, browsing through the ones she didn't recognize the contents of, got to work on sorting them.

Creating a plan, so she didn't have to leave the library a mess while she worked, she removed and replaced various books, shifting their locations by subject then author. Now and then she covertly glanced back at the Duke who was working on his own projects at his desk. He seemed to ignore her presence which suited her well.

Ria jumped, startled when a maid knocked and then opened the door at the Duke's assent. She carried a tray with a pot of tea and small pastries into the room and placed it in a corner, glancing at Ria, and then leaving the room. The Duke stood as Ria walked over to the pot of tea, "Allow me, Your

Grace." He nodded and sat in front of the fire. She fixed a cup of tea and brought it to him.

"Thank you, Miss Victoria," he said as she handed it to him.

"Ria," she replied automatically then blushed. She cleared her throat and continued, "People only call me Victoria when I'm in trouble."

He laughed jovially, "Miss Ria then." He considered for a moment grimacing, "No, there's something about that which doesn't sound right. Just Ria."

 Watching her, his eyes unreadable, he said, "In that case, you must call me Andres."

Her eyes widened, afraid she was about to run away, he followed with, "At least in private while you're working on the library."

She relaxed and smiled then went to fix her own cup of tea, joining him in front of the fire. They spoke of the books she had borrowed and their favorite genres.

Ria's head flew up when the clock chimed the five o'clock hour. Time had flown by, and she needed to leave before someone missed her at home. She smiled at Andres, growing more confident during their conversation, "I must be going."

"When will you come again?"

She considered, picking up a book she had set aside, "The day after tomorrow?" He nodded his assent and walked her to the library door.

"Would you like me to walk with you to the front door?"

"That's unnecessary," she replied, bobbing her head as she fled the room. He watched her until she rounded the corner of the hall.

Over the next few weeks, their association continued in the same manner, growing more comfortable with each other in private though she avoided him during public gatherings.

Chapter 3

s spring took hold of the city, the walks to the Duke's townhouse grew more pleasant. The house staff greeted Ria with happiness when she came to visit though today the butler pulled her aside before she could make her way to the back of the house.

"I wanted to warn you, he's in something of a bad humor," he said. She looked past him, towards the library, and took a deep breath.

"Thank you for telling me," she said, smiling at the butler. He nodded to her as she walked down the hall towards the library. She tapped on the door and frowned when she received no response. Opening it, she looked through the portal, seeing Andres standing with his back to the room, looking out the French doors towards the garden.

"May I come in?" she asked, tentatively.

He turned towards her, a thunderous look on his face, but nodded. She entered, not having seen him this upset since the first night they met, and closed the door behind her. Instead of bothering him, she walked over to the bookcase she had been working on and looked through the tomes.

Pacing around his desk, he looked between her and the floor in front of him, shaking his fingers in an agitated manner. He stopped and looked at her again, frowning as he said to her, "You're not going to ask what's wrong?".

"I figured you'd tell me in your own time if it was something you wanted to share," she replied, not looking at him. He continued to frown at her, watching her sort through the books. She tried not to be self-conscious as he watched her intently, feeling like they had moved past that point.

"Come play chess with me," he said, turning and walking towards a chess set sitting in front of a window. Comfortable armchairs flanked the game, inviting players to sink into them. She took a chair across from him on the white side.

The pieces, crafted from smooth marble, sat on a gorgeous wooden board inlaid with light and dark wood with stone around the perimeter. Ria ran her fingers over the outside of the board admiring it. She picked up the king, looking at the features carved with a meticulous and skilled hand.

"That's the king," Andres said, "He moves one space at a time." She raised an eyebrow, placing the king back on the board. Smiling, she allowed him to explain how to play the game to her without comment. "The white side plays first."

Ria picked up a pawn, the fourth one from the right, and moved it forward two spaces. Andres smiled at her and copied the move with the same pawn on his side, blocking her from being able to move forward another space. She looked up at him, her hand hovering over her pieces as if she was undecided on how to continue. Biting her lower lip, she picked up her kingside bishop and moved it to the same level as her pawn.

"So, are you going to tell me what's wrong?" she asked as he picked up his queenside knight and placed it into play.

"The Americans are acting up again, threatening war. It puts me in a hard place because I own property across England, France, Spain, and in the Americas. With England fighting Bonaparte in France, and Spain looking like it will enter the fray soon, it's a mess. I'm tired of straddling the fence between all of them. I found out yesterday that the American Navy has commandeered several of my trade ships."

Ria grimaced, wishing she had knowledge of politics which could help him through this ordeal. She picked up her queen and moved it as far as she could to the right side of the board.

"I need to speak with the Marquess of Townshend. The old recluse refuses to meet with even me," he said, bitterness tinging his voice. "He needs to understand the consequences of allowing his holdings to fall into ruin. Unfortunately, his heir is a dandy with no business sense or care for his people." Picking up his queenside pawn, he moved it forward one space.

"Lord Townshend is a member of the Royal Institution; he never misses a meeting. I believe the next one is on Thursday afternoon," she replied, picking up her queen and moving it along the diagonal to take the kingside pawn, "Also, check and mate."

Andres stared at the board speechless, then looked up at her. "I thought you didn't know how to play."

"I never said I didn't know how to play. You assumed," she smiled, "My grandfather taught me when I was still in the nursery. We play almost every night before retiring for the evening." He sat back in his chair and crossed his arms over his chest. He wasn't wearing a waistcoat, preferring a more comfortable and casual attire for home, and his biceps bulged against the thin fabric covering them. Ria tried not to focus on them, trying not to give away her attraction as she reset the board for another game.

"This time, don't go easy on me." She gave him a one-sided smile as she took the first move. While he moved his piece in response, she said, "As for Lord Townshend, I may be able to help you." He glanced up at her, giving her his full attention.

"Entrance into the Institution is by invitation only. However, members are allowed to bring guests at their own discretion," she smiled at him, taking her turn.

"So, you believe you know someone who will help me gain entrance to the institute?"

"My grandfather is a member, and I believe a good friend of Lord Townshend. I am sure he would be happy to recommend you if you were to call on him in the morning and mention your interest. I'm surprised you aren't a member already."

He waved a hand in dismissal, "I have more memberships to clubs and institutes than I could ever use. I'm sure I received an invitation at one time."

They played two more games, Andres's mood improved significantly when he beat her the last time. Ria watched him while they played. The fading light of the sun fell across his face, lighting his features and casting away the imposing shadows which lingered earlier. Never seeming to get enough of his company, she hoped he didn't see her interest. She didn't want to ruin the tentative companionship they had formed.

"Tomorrow," she said with a smile as she stood to take her leave.

"Tomorrow," he replied, watching her go.

Andres sat back in his chair as her skirts disappeared around the door and brought his thumbnail to his teeth. He contemplated the information she had given him and decided he would call on her grandfather the next afternoon though he had a busy schedule. He moved as many tasks as possible to the days she wasn't visiting so he could be there while she was. Sighing, he flicked his fingers and then tapped them on the arm of the chair.

She fascinated him as no other woman did. Brilliant and witty, her smile lit up the room on even the dreariest of days. He found himself unable to focus on his work while she wasn't there, too busy listening for her footsteps down the hall to concentrate. His servants had nothing but good things to say about her. Growling, he shook his head. He was looking forward to seeing her altogether too much.

Chapter 4

ia sat in the parlor before the grand piano, staring at the keys. It was midafternoon, and she had finished the book she'd brought home with her the night before. Calling hours were almost over, with a small meal following promptly. Her family was attending the opera that evening and would stop by an eatery before.

She wasn't invited and would stay home. Lydia decreed that Lacey needed to be the center of attention and Ria would only distract from her. They couldn't have her awkward cousin reminding every one of their family's shame. Andres hadn't appeared to see her grandfather yet, though she tried to pretend she wasn't waiting for him.

Running her fingers over the ivory keys, she played a haunting melody she had created herself. Few people knew she could play the piano. It was a skill she was private about, not having the courage to play in front of others who might judge her.

Closing her eyes, she felt her way through the music; the notes coming more from her heart than her fingers. She placed all of her feelings into the music, releasing through it the words that her mouth could not.

Andres watched her play from the doorway. She never registered his presence, not even when the butler had quietly announced him trying not to disturb her. He was sure what he was seeing was special. The music spoke to him and drew him closer like a moth to a flame. He didn't realize he was walking towards her until a woman came brushing past him, releasing him from the siren song.

"Victoria! Stop that racket at once!" Lydia yelled as she came into the room. Deep inside of the music, her cousin-in-law startled her, causing her to play a jarring note before she removed her fingers from the keys. She clenched her hands into fists, placing them in her lap.

"I'm sorry Your Grace, my cousin is a rather odd woman," Lydia said. Victoria spun around wide-eyed, wondering how long he had been standing there. She noticed the glare he was shooting at the back of Lydia's head as she walked in front of him and hid a smile.

"You play beautifully, My Lady."

"She's not a Lady, and I'm sure she will excuse herself in a moment; however, Miss Lacey will be right down," Lydia said, beaming.

"Who?" he looked from one woman to the other, confused.

Victoria stood, folding her hands in front of her, "I believe Grandfather mentioned that His Grace might stop by to speak with him."

"Your grandfather is resting before the opera tonight, we must not disturb him," Lydia snapped at her.

"Then perhaps I will see him, and all of you, there," Andres responded. His tone was polite, but she could see the fire in his eyes as he looked at Lydia. She would not want to be on the receiving end of that stare.

"You're attending the opera tonight, Your Grace?" Lydia asked, not noticing his gaze.

"Of course."

Looking at the ground, her eyes sad, "Unfortunately, I—" Ria started to say.

"Victoria isn't invited, but I look forward to seeing you this evening, Your Grace," Lacey said from behind him. Andres turned, backing up and letting her pass, his expression unreadable. She curtsied with grace Ria would never have and gave him a flirtatious yet proper smile. A new gown of lightest pink silk, trimmed with delicate white ribbons, flattered her statuesque figure. Victoria tried not to compare her faded and worn morning dress to the younger girl's outfit. He nodded in return, not saying anything to her.

"I must speak to your grandfather," he said, turning back to Lydia, "Why don't you join me in my box tonight? Your whole family." He emphasized the word *whole* while gesturing to include Ria in the invitation. "I've heard this opera is fascinating and I believe everyone should have the chance to see it. My grandmother is joining me. I'm sure she would be delighted to meet you." He was speaking to Lydia, but she knew the words were meant for her. Ria's eyes flicked up and caught his. He gave her an intense look and turned to leave. "I'll send a carriage for you at five o'clock."

As Andres mounted his horse, he smiled to himself; the evening ahead looked like it would be less tedious then he expected.

At five o'clock sharp, a carriage with the Duke's emblem on it arrived in front of their townhouse. People stopped to stare as they left their home and entered the carriage. Ria had spoken to her grandfather in private and explained what Andres wanted. Her grandfather would expect to have a conversation about the Institution with Andres later in the evening.

In turn, her grandfather had told her stories about growing up with the Duke's grandfather and the Grand Duchess which amused her to no end. She wondered if Andres would find the stories interesting as well.

A short ride through the streets of London and they arrived at one of the best eateries in the city, across the street from the Opera House. As they walked in, Ria again tried not to dwell on not meeting the standards of these people even though she was wearing her best gown. The maître d'hôtel looked down on her and sneered but said nothing as he led them back to a table where the Andres and his grandmother waited.

As she saw them, the Grand Duchess's face lit up, and she stood. Walking around the table, she made a beeline for Ria. "Miss Victoria, when my grandson said others were joining us for the evening, I never imagined it would be your family!"

She took Ria's face in her hands, beaming as she kissed her on both cheeks. Ria couldn't tell which was more amusing, the shock on Andres's face or the disgust on Lydia's.

Ria beamed at her, "I've missed seeing you, Lady Marie. We have so much to catch up on. I'd no idea you were back in town."

"I arrived earlier this week. I had planned on sending you a card, but I fear time has gotten away from me," Lady Marie answered.

"As it seems my manners have left me," Ria replied, placing her arm through Lady Marie's and leading her over to her family. "You know my grandfather and cousin Christian. I'm not sure you've met my cousin's wife, Lady Lydia. They married just after the Season ended last year." Lydia nodded to Lady Marie while glaring daggers at Ria.

"And Lady Lydia's younger sister, Miss Lacey. This is her first Season, and from what I've heard, she's made quite the splash," she said as Lady Marie gave her a quizzical look. Ria shrugged in response, giving Lydia and Lacey a sweet smile. Lacey, oblivious to the undercurrents of the conversation, curtsied to the Duchess who inclined her head in response.

After the greetings were over, they sat at the table. Lady Marie had insisted Ria sit between her and Andres with her grandfather on the other side so Lady Marie could catch up with him. Next to her grandfather sat Lydia and then Christian, with Lacey between him and Andres on the other side, which pleased Lydia to no end.

Lacey kept up a constant stream of chatter which Andres, due to social convention, wasn't able to ignore. In answer to the inane questions she asked him, he responded with single syllable words. Christian made no move to speak with the girl, instead choosing to stare into the bottom of his brandy.

Ria observed the others. Lydia was talking to Christian, complaining about one thing or another, while he grunted in response. He swirled the amber liquid in his glass. Lady Marie and her grandfather had their heads bent together, reminiscing about their younger days she assumed.

She looked around Andres towards Lacey, her eyebrow raised, and said, "Isn't that Lord Heyworth sitting at that table over there?"

Lacey turned to scan the room, preening when she found the gentleman in question. He was looking around his mother, watching her with rapt attention.

Andres turned to her, "Thank you, no, seriously." She pursed her lips to hide a grin and poked him in the leg under the table. He chuckled and turned towards her. "Tell me, how do you know my grandmother?"

"She and my grandmother were good friends," she said, smiling with fondness towards the woman. She leaned closer to Andres. "Grandmother used to take me with her to visit Lady Marie when I was younger. She used to give me sweets when I would correctly recite poems from her favorite books. When my grandmother passed away, Lady Marie was there to comfort me."

Tears filled her eyes at the memory of her beloved grandmother, but she blinked them away before they could fall. Andres was watching her with an indistinguishable look on his face. He reached under the table and ran his hand over her knuckles in a comforting gesture, allowing his fingers to linger. Ria smiled at him. Taking a deep breath, she continued, "Now I help her pick the books for her book club and visit with her while she is in town."

Andres watched her, his heart squeezing when he saw her distress. It surprised him to find out his grandmother knew her. Most women wouldn't keep an advantageous society connection hidden from others, but Ria had never tried to use it to her advantage. She also never tried to use her association with him to her advantage. It was a rare quality in the ton.

They finished dinner, her and Andres conversing pleasantly while Lacey eye-flirted with Lord Heyworth across the room. Their party moved across the street to the theater, mounting the stairs to Andres's box. Ushers added extra chairs to accommodate their members, and the theater darkened as the grand opera began.

Ria sat to the far left in the front of the box with Lacey next to her. Lydia and Christian sat next to them completing the first row. Andres, sitting behind her, tickled the back of her neck with a fan while his grandmother leaned over to speak with her grandfather. They seemed to be in their own world, oblivious to the goings-on around them.

Glaring over her shoulder at him, she couldn't help but notice the boyish grin he wore. She rolled her eyes and turned back to the performance, using glasses to get a better view of the stage. She felt tickling at the back of her neck again sending shivers down her spine. Reaching back, she rubbed the spot as he suppressed laughter behind her.

Andres continued to torture her through the first act and into the second. Finally, Ria had enough and pretended to play with a strand of her hair that had fallen out of its bindings. As he reached forward to tickle the back of her neck again, she snatched the fan from his grasp. She opened it and used it to fan herself lazily, grinning over her shoulder at him. Glaring back, he pouted in the most adorable way. Turning around, she laughed to herself and shook her head. Behind her, she heard an "Oomph," and a hissed "Behave" which she assumed came from his grandmother. Stifling a smile, she watched the opera.

Intermission came sooner than she would have liked, the half-hour between acts of the opera a time for people to visit and catch up. It seemed as though her grandfather had many friends who wanted to speak with him, but Andres pulled him aside. She watched the men speak to each other, their heads bent together and smiled, looking away.

Lydia walked up to her and said, "I think His Grace is quite taken with Lacey." Ria looked at her and continued to smile. She knew Andres had no interest in Lacey but didn't want to say anything to Lydia for fear of the repercussions the harpy that would lay upon her.

"I believe Lord Heyworth has caught her fancy," Ria said.

Lydia glared at the man talking to her younger sister, and said, "A Viscount is not good enough for my sister." Ria raised an eyebrow. She thought a donkey was too good for Lacey. She chided herself for thinking such horrible thoughts.

The Viscount left, and Lacey came over to them, sneering. "I'm amazed they even let you in here Victoria. Even the peasants in the lower pews are better dressed than you are."

Ria reassessed her earlier thoughts. A roach was too good for her cousin-in-law's sister. Before she formulated a scathing retort, an actor came onto the stage to announce the end of intermission. As they took their seats, she glanced over her shoulder to see Andres glaring at Lydia. She hoped he hadn't heard what she said, embarrassed although there was nothing she could do about her situation.

Andres sat fuming at the little nitwit in front of him. It saddened him that the rest of society judged Ria because of how much money she had and what her titles or lack thereof were. Sighing he realized that he would do the same thing if he didn't know her so well from their private conversations. That didn't mean she needed a constant reminder from the people she lived with. It was no wonder she came so often to the townhouse to escape them. At least he could give her that for now, he would have to think of a better solution for the future.

Sitting cross-legged on the floor of the second story, in the corner nearest the door, Ria watched Andres working at his desk. He had been in good humor that morning, his meeting with Lord Townshend having gone well the previous evening. He was going over the ledgers from one of his French estates, glaring at the pages while running his fingers through his hair.

Ria smiled, clutching an open book to her chest. His hair would become a mess, but he didn't seem to notice. She found that she loved watching him, growing fonder by the day. Uncertain if he would still allow her to visit after she finished the library, she worked slower than she had previously to eke out as much time with him as possible.

Jumping as the loud crash of the door being thrown opened below startled her, Ria glanced over the railing as an unknown but furious man entered the room. He wore a bright blue coat over matching pantaloons and white stockings. The edges of the coat and side seams of the pants had ostentatious embroidery, his outfit crying for attention all dandies craved. Complete with shined boots, a top hat, and pristine teal cravat, Ria thought the man looked ridiculous when he removed his hat to reveal curling brown hair shot through with gray.

She moved back against the bookcase, making herself as small as possible against the shelves and thanking her lucky stars she had worn a brown dress that day. She saw Andres's eyes flick up to her as he stood from his desk, his manner calm and face impassive.

Focusing on the man approaching him, Andres said, "Lord Townshend, you would come barging into my home? Explain yourself."

"You went to my father last night. I told you no one was to bother him and yet you went to speak to him anyhow," Lord Townshend was sputtering with anger. He started ranting, and Andres cut him off with a glare and a hand motion.

"You dare use that tone when speaking with me?" The Duke asked the man in a steady yet menacing tone.

If was as if a switch had flipped in Lord Townshend. Suddenly, he stopped talking, tensing as Andres walked around the desk towards him in a slow, stalking manner. She wasn't able to hear what Andres was saying to him, his tone dropping lower than she could pick up from the upper floor.   His demeanor, however, was that of a predator whose lunch had just run in front of him. He had a lot of anger he needed to release over the Townshend matter, and it seemed he had found his target.

Ria moved low and crawled towards the railing, peeking over the side through the rails. Lord Townshend was cowering before Andres, and she swore the man was shaking. Andres's eyes flicked up to her again, and she moved back just before he motioned the other Lord to leave his house, instructing the butler to lead him out. She knew Winston, she had learned his name after considerable cajoling, had much the same expression as his master. Hoping that he wouldn't get in trouble for allowing the other man past him, she went down the spiral staircase and walked over to Andres' desk.

Back straight and hands planted on the surface of the desk, Andres had his eyes closed as he took deep calming breaths. She leaned against the desk next to his arm. Reaching out, she ran her fingers through his hair at his temple. He stiffened for a moment but then turned his face into her hand and let her continue, releasing his pent-up anger in a final exhale.

"What can I do to help you?" she asked him, her voice gentle.

He brought his hands up and rubbed his face, looking at the book in front of him, and gave a forced laugh, "You can tell me what's wrong with these ledgers."

"Move over," she said even though she believed he was half joking. Perhaps it was something she could help him with.

He moved the chair back so she could stand in front of him and look over the ledger. After a few minutes of her standing there, she felt his arms wrap around her waist from behind as he pulled her down to sit in his lap. A small shiver ran down her spine as she tried not to think too far into the meaning of the embrace. She assumed he just wanted her to be more comfortable than standing there in front of him, that was sure to be it.

Andres held onto the scrap of a woman in front of him, enjoying her soft curves though he would never say so. She was soft, and she fit well into his embrace. He laid his head on her shoulder, breathing in her personal scent of lavender and mint. Positioning her so she wouldn't feel his improper intentions behind her, he savored the warmth of holding her in his arms. What he was doing was wrong, he was taking liberties that no woman should allow, but she seemed not to mind. Ria gave a small sound of dissent and rapidly flipped back and forth between several pages. He could see her running her long and agile fingers down the columns over her shoulder as she mumbled to herself.

"I expect, this is mere speculation mind, that your steward has been skimming off the top of the profits from the sale of livestock..." she said, turning her head towards his, their faces mere inches apart. Her breath caught in her throat as her eyes met his. Tilting his chin, a little higher his gaze fell to her tender lips which were parted ever so slightly, begging for a kiss. Andres smiled as he tilted his head, he wanted to see if she tasted as sweet as she smelled.

"This is adorable. It really is."

Ria gasped and jumped off of Andres's lap, moving to the other side of the room, her face blazing red. He watched her with regret and then turned to his brother who had just entered the room.

"What do you want, Vince?"

"Oh, the usual: money, women, and fast horses. Not necessarily in that order, of course," Vince replied, flopping into the chair across from the desk and placing his feet on an ottoman while grinning across the table at Andres.

"Ria, you know my brother Vince, I'm sure."

"Ria?" Vince winked at him.

He glared back at his brother, the pest loved nothing better to tease him, but he wasn't keen on the idea of him treating her the same way. "Stop."

"Townshend the younger is on his way to see you, I figured I would warn you beforehand," Vince said.

"You are too late by an hour at least," Andres replied, sitting back in his chair and running his hands over the armrests.

"What did he have to say?"

"The usual sputtering and indignant tirade," Andres replied, frowning.

"And?" Vince raised an eyebrow, studying his brother.

"I took care of it," Andres shrugged in response, "Hopefully, we will see improvement on that front."

Ria watched the two from the window seat in the corner. She did not understand what had almost happened, but she was sure she would have enjoyed it. Andres seemed interested in her, but she knew it was impossible, he was too far above her station to ever consider a relationship with her. She needed to keep that in mind for the future and try not to let him too close. Any relationship she had with him would only end in disaster and tears.

"You said you noticed something in the books?" Andres asked her.

Clearing her throat, she walked back over to his desk, more composed now she'd gotten over her initial embarrassment. She hoped he wouldn't notice the flurry of emotions that moved under the surface of her calm façade.

"I was saying, I think your steward for these holdings is skimming profits. If you look back, even three years, the profits have gone down almost twenty percent for this estate. However, if you look at the closest neighboring estate you own, profits on the sale of livestock have increased steadily over the last few years. Obviously, some difference can be attributed..." she looked at Vince who was staring at her wide-eyed, "What?"

He shook his head, blinking and laughed, "I've just never met a lady like you."

Ria narrowed her eyes at him. She couldn't tell if he was making fun of her or being serious.

"Regardless, guess where you get to go," Andres said grinning at him with a malicious glint in his eye.

"No. I refuse."

"You don't have a choice, it's either go or stay here to plan the winter ball with Grandmother while I go to France. The invitations go out the last week of Season, and I know she's already on top of the list."

Glowering, Vince growled, "Fine." He stood up, offering Ria his hand. She frowned but put her hand in his. Running his lips across the back of her knuckles, he winked at her, "Until we meet again, my fair maiden. Know you hold my heart in your sweet hands."

Ria groaned and rolled her eyes, making a show of wiping the back of her hand off on her skirts, much to Andres's amusement. Vince laughed as he took his leave to prepare for his journey.

"Where are you sending him?"

"To speak with our steward and discuss the issues with our declining livestock profits," he said smiling at her over the desk. "Thank you. I think I've looked at these numbers for so long they all became the same."

"It sounds like you need to take a break," she said, holding her hand out to him. A hopeful look crossed his face, and as he stood, she said, "Let's play a game of chess." If she wasn't mistaken, she could have sworn that a disappointed grimace replaced the previous look. If it had been there, it flickered away in an instant as he took her hand and let her lead him over to the chess set.

Chapter 5

*I*t had been almost two weeks since she had last seen Andres and Ria was itching to go to the townhouse now he was back in London. At first, she wasn't able to make it to his house because of the social obligations Lydia had placed her under. She hadn't been feeling well and charged Ria with chaperoning Lacey to most of the events the sisters attended.

Then, when Lydia felt well enough to take back her duties, Andres had to leave town on business for a week. She had found out he returned because he had attended one of the dinner parties that her family attended.

He never approached her as that would be considered impolite and could cause gossip, but more than once she felt his eyes following her around the room. Due to the surprise at his presence at the dinner, she wondered if he had attended solely to let her know he was back in town for lack of other means.

Lydia and Lacey were attending a luncheon at another residence for the afternoon which meant that Ria could escape once they left. Lydia, dressed and ready to go to the event, walked into the room, frowning at Ria as she commonly did.

"There you are," she said as Ria looked up at her, "I've been looking all over for you. Lady Marie is hosting a recital on Thursday morning, and I would like you to obtain an invitation for Lacey."

Ria frowned, "I'm sorry, but I can't do that. I would never presume to ask the Duchess for an invitation to one of her events."

"You seemed friendly enough with her."

"That's not the point. I love her like a grandmother, but I have no social standing to ask her for an invitation," Ria replied, frowning with a fierce look on her face.

"Regardless, Lacey must attend that recital. If you can't get an invitation then, honestly, what good are you? Perhaps it's time for you to go back home to Thornbridge."

Ria's mouth dropped open in astonishment, "Are you threatening me?"

"Of course not," Lydia said with a smug smile curling across her lips, "I think you should have better care and appreciation for the quality of life you have here. I also don't think you should have any issues securing the invitation. I know your mother would love for you to come home on a more permanent basis otherwise." With that, Lydia flounced from the room not paying any attention to the deadly glare aimed at her back.

Andres felt like he had been waiting all morning for Ria to appear. He had tried to bury himself in his work, but he was too excited. A brand new grand piano sat in one of the unoccupied corners of the library. He had ordered it specifically for her. The piano had been tuned to perfection earlier that week, and he couldn't wait to hear her play again. One taste of the music she created wasn't enough.

When she entered the room, and he stood up to greet her, he knew that something was wrong. Her lips pursed, she was wearing a dark look on her face he'd never seen before. As mad as she seemed, she still took care when placing the books she borrowed back on the shelves.

He walked over to her, taking her into his arms and holding her. At first, she was stiff but then she let out a great sigh and relaxed against him. Placing her cheek on his chest, she wrapped her arms around his waist. He laid his chin on the top of her head.

He held her like that for several minutes before nuzzling her hair and asking, "What's wrong? Tell me."

"It's nothing," she replied, breathing in the pine and leather smell that surrounded him. He must have been walking out in the gardens earlier that morning since he still smelled of spring forests. She took pleasure in the warmth that spread from his chest, closing her eyes and savoring the closeness, the security in his embrace.

"Such a female answer," he said teasing her while rubbing her back, eliciting a chuckle and pinch to his side from her in response. "Tell me."

Ria groaned, "My lovely cousin has decided that she needs to move up in her social circle and has demanded an invitation to Lady Marie's upcoming recital. She refuses to take no for an answer. I refuse to use my association with your grandmother for such pandering."

"I don't believe that's all," he said, considering her. She wouldn't be this mad if her cousin demanded a simple invitation to a gathering which she refused to provide. He felt her stiffen in his arms before sighing.

"She implied that if I can't procure the requested invitation, then I have no worth to her and perhaps it is time I go back to my father's house in Thornbridge."

Andres stood still. Thornbridge was far to the north, almost to the Scottish border. The thought of not seeing her again, never playing chess with her or being able to speak so freely with her, did something to his chest he couldn't describe.

"I plan to attend the recital. I can secure your family an invitation."

"No, I won't take advantage of our friendship that way," she said, shaking her head against his chest.

Releasing her, he placed his finger under her chin and tilted her head up. Her sad eyes met his, and he would do anything to cheer her. He knew her pride wouldn't let her take anything from him, even an invitation to an event he could easily procure.

"Then a trade perhaps?"

Ria perked up though she was afraid of what he would ask. "What kind of trade?"

"Grandmother's recitals are the talk of society because she always finds the most talented musicians to play for her gathering. Take a turn at the piano. Play as you did the morning before the opera."

"I can't... I don't..." she stuttered, a look of fear crossing her face. "Never."

Taking her by the hand, Andres led her to the piano. The dark wood of the meticulously polished case reflected her stunned expression as she admired the instrument. He brought her to the bench and sat her on it as she still seemed shocked to see the piano before her. With care, she ran her fingers over the keys, pressing different ones to test the trueness of the pitch. Her eyebrows raised at the sweet sound the piano created. She placed her other hand next to her first on the keyboard and plucked a slow and wistful melody.

Andres sat next to her, taking the lower half of the keyboard, and played a few chords. Smiling at him, Ria adjusted her playing to match his. They played together, neither speaking but rather enjoying the music and the company of one another. Andres removed his hands from the keyboard and flattened them on the bench, letting her take over. For what seemed like an eternity, she played what she felt, releasing her pent-up emotions through the music. He sat there, making no sound, rather watching her and reveling in the beauty of her music. Playing the final notes, she balled her hands into fists and removed them from the keyboard.

"You can," he said, his voice soft, as she stared at the keys. She looked up at him in silence, letting her gaze linger before looking back down at the keyboard, and nodded.

A butler greeted Ria, Lydia, and Lacey at the door and he showed them into the grand parlor of the Duchess' town residence. The two-story room was tastefully decorated with gold-trimmed, light cream furniture. The inlaid marble floors held several pillars situated around the perimeter of the room to support a viewing gallery on the second floor. Each set of pillars contained an arched window between them to allow natural lighting. A grand piano stood at one end with chairs arranged in front of it for observers. Other instruments including a harp, violin, and flute stood ready on stands around it. Through large glass doors into another room, Ria glimpsed banquet tables laid out with delicate pastries and savories for the guests.

She clenched her hands together and tried not to let her nerves show. Lady Marie had stopped by the day before during visiting hours to extend their family an invitation to the event and Ria had refused to meet her eye. She was embarrassed that she was used in such a way and didn't want the Duchess to see the shame coloring her face.

Andres looked away from the conversation he was having with Lady Averherst and her daughter when Ria and her family entered. She was wearing what he found out was her best dress, but he couldn't help but observe the sneers of the women standing next to him. He was about to comment until he realized that their looks weren't directed at Ria, but at her cousins.

"What are they doing here?" the younger girl asked her mother.

"Social climbers. It's disturbing."

"Grandmother told me that Miss Victoria is an accomplished musician," Andres added to the conversation.

"Poor girl, having to put up with those two," Lady Averherst said, "I imagine if Lady Marie asked her to play there is no chance they would let her attend alone."

If you only knew, Andres thought, frowning.

Excusing himself from the group, he went to find his grandmother. Since Ria's group had arrived later than was fashionable, everyone had been waiting for them to begin the recital and Lady Marie wasn't pleased.

Ria separated herself from Lydia and Lacey and went in search of Lady Marie. Finding her in the room where the food was being served, talking to a group of women, Ria stood a polite distance away until the ladies finished their conversation.

"You're late, very late," Lady Marie said with a stern look.

Ria spread her hands in a defeated gesture, her eyes sad. Before she could speak, she heard Andres over her shoulder, "I assume it wasn't her fault."

"Yes, usually her punctuality is impeccable," Lady Marie replied, her demeanor softening. "My grandson tells me you were coerced into attending today."

Eyes flicking to where Lydia and Lacey were trying to insert themselves into a conversation with others who didn't seem to welcome them, Ria said, "I'm not quite ready for fresh country air." Lady Marie sniffed, following her gaze.

"Let's start, shall we?" she asked.

A shiver ran down Ria's spine, and she said, "If we must."

Andres gave his grandmother his arm and led her into the main room, Ria following a decent distance behind them. Taking one of the front seats with the other performers, she watched as Lady Marie welcomed all those in attendance with an elegant grace and introduced the first musician. A hush fell over the crowd as she played the violin, showcasing the talents that earned her the first spot in the lineup.

All the women sat in chairs, but the men stood in groups around the room. Andres stood on the other side of the instruments which meant that she was facing him, now and when she would be playing. In too short of a time, it was her turn. The Duchess introduced her, gesturing for her to take her place at the piano.

With trepidation, she sat before the keyboard. Pandering to the gathering, she played an easy sonata, a popular one that everyone knew. She heard whispers behind her, and her confidence lagged. Andres walked over to the piano, placing his hands on the case, and leaning down so he could stare her in the eyes. The whispering grew frenzied. They had kept their friendship from the ton, but she felt that wouldn't be the case any longer.

Ria stopped playing and curled her fingers, numb from cold and nerves, into her palms then looked up at him. He raised an eyebrow at her, and she sighed in response. She knew what he wanted. Cracking her neck and rolling her shoulders, she placed her fingers back on the keyboard and ignored the people behind her. After releasing a deep breath, she played the sonata she had written, the one he had walked in on that first day. Her confidence grew, and she let go, letting the music flow from her heart and through her fingers.

Andres stood up and stepped back to his position along the wall, sure that Ria didn't notice. Though hesitant at first, her playing soon overtook the room. No one uttered a sound as her fingers flew across the keys playing the same siren song that had drawn him to her that first afternoon. He would never tire of hearing it, never tire of the emotions it stirred in his heart.

The room was silent, rapt with attention though she didn't know it from her position, as she played the last few keys. Ria placed her hands back in her lap, afraid to turn around, afraid to see the condemnation in the faces of the Lords and Ladies gathered. Someone clapped, and it was as if a dam burst. Suddenly, a roar of applause filled the small room and, as Ria turned, people stood. Her face turning red, she stood to curtsy to them, then ran for the door. She wasn't used to praise and didn't know how to handle it.

Chapter 6

Ria had spent a miserable weekend with Lydia and Lacey, their constant torment grating on her nerves. Neither could believe she had made such an impression on the gathering at the recital, but they had received several visitors who wished to praise her for her skill.

Lacey was very resentful about not being the center of attention. Though several of the ladies at the party thought she should not be among them, her beauty caught the eye of one or two wealthy noblemen who had arranged introductions. Lydia seemed more concerned with Ria's association with Andres and wouldn't stop asking her insinuating questions.

It was Monday morning, and the women were about to leave for a luncheon. After the recital, Ria had told her grandfather what happened over a game of chess. He was infuriated over the subterfuge and had spoken with Christian. The aftereffect was that her grandfather and Christian told Lydia to leave her alone. She wasn't to coerce or strong-arm Ria into any commands she found unreasonable.

Lydia had thrown a fit, railing against the injustice of their demands and screaming that she was the Countess. She became livid when their grandfather reminded her that she wasn't, in fact, the Countess because he was still alive. There had been screaming, tears, and broken vases, but her grandfather refused to back down. Ria knew this wasn't the last they would hear of it and could only wonder at what revenge Lydia would take. Hiding in her room, Ria watched out the front window to see the carriage leave before starting her day.

It was a warm afternoon in mid-May, birdsong filled the air, and Ria took a deep calming breath as she walked to Andres's townhouse. The sounds of the city surrounding her disrupted the serenity of the day, but brought her closer to the life that constantly flowed through the streets. She took the time to savor her freedom. If there were benefits to not having titles and a large dowry, this was one of them. She had the freedom to be herself without the strict expectations of Society. Being invisible didn't hurt either.

Reaching her destination, she rang the bell and gave the butler a cheery greeting upon being admitted to the residence. She said good afternoon to the maids as she passed them and complimented the girl who was dusting in the hall with a smile.

After the first few weeks of visiting the Duke's household, Ria was surprised the gossip of her trips hadn't spread. The housekeeper, a kind older woman, assured Ria that they respected her and the Duke too much to spread their business to the other households. She appreciated their discretion.

Walking into the library with a good afternoon for Andres, she did not expect to find him with company. Lady Marie looked at her over the corner of the couch and smiled. Ria relaxed when she realized who his guest was.

She walked over to Lady Marie and sat next to her on the couch where she had indicated.

"My guests were most impressed with your performance, my dear," she said, smiling. "Even I didn't know you could play so well."

Andres, who was sitting in the armchair across from them, grinned at his grandmother. "I told you to have faith. Have I ever steered you wrong before?"

"I can admit when you are right. She will be perfect."

"For what?" Ria asked with confusion. "I'm not playing in any more recitals."

Andres laughed, shaking his head, "No. We would like to ask you to become Grandmother's companion through the end of the year. She is planning a large end-of-year event at Alnwick Castle and needs help."

Ria sat back and considered their proposal. Generally, a companion lived with the Lady she served, but she didn't want to move away from her grandfather. Aside from that, she saw nothing wrong with the offer.

"I can't leave my grandfather," she responded.

Lady Marie smiled, taking her hand, "I wouldn't expect you to. You can continue to live in your grandfather's house and come here to use the library. We will plan the event from here, and you will have to come on a daily basis. We have much to do and little time to do it in. We will have to leave by the last week of October in order to reach the country manor in time. The event will start on the first of December though I'm sure people will arrive in the two weeks prior. It will end on the first of January at which point, depending on the weather, we will travel back to London."

"In return for your service, I will provide you with a complete wardrobe," Andres chimed in. "And, of course, we will take care of all of your travel and accommodations."

"That's too much," Ria said in shock, looking at him and his grandmother.

"It's what is expected of you as the companion to the Duchess," he replied in a matter-of-fact way that brooked no argument. "You will also accompany my grandmother to all of her events, though she rarely attends." Ria nodded her understanding.

"Wouldn't the Duchess, Andres's mother, be helping?" she asked.

Shaking his head, Andres replied, "My mother hates England. When my father passed away, and I took the titles, she took my younger sisters and moved back to Spain to be near her family. That was several years ago, and she hasn't been back since." Ria realized that must be where he got is darker, more exotic, looks from.

"It's settled then!" said Lady Marie, beaming. "I will call my seamstress and have her come by the end of the week to get started on your wardrobe. You need at least five morning dresses, four afternoon dresses, two ball gowns, or perhaps three. I think we should have at least one ready for the last ball of this season..." and she continued through the long list of items she would need. Andres grew bored and went back to his own work.

Ria watched the excited older woman and realized it was something she had wanted to do for a long time but never had the excuse. Glancing at Andres, she couldn't help but note the smile that played over his lips. She looked back at Lady Marie, "... and you will need to learn all the new waltzes so we will have to call the dance master."

"Waltzes?" Ria asked in shock, her eyebrows raised. They had just come into fashion, Society matrons still thinking them too risqué.

"Yes well, even if we don't end up dancing one at the balls, you should still learn." Lady Marie said with a sly grin. She patted Ria's knee and then stood. "I must be off. I will meet you here tomorrow morning to prune the guest list and write invitations. I'd like to have them out by the second week of June before everyone leaves for the country."

Setting down the quill she was holding, Ria flexed her hand. Her fingers were sore but, after days of writing, she had finished the invitations and was ready to seal them after Lady Marie checked them. They had spent most of the week deciding on who would attend the winter getaway, cutting the list from around seventy different families to just over forty. Ria thought there would be a lot of upset nobles, but that wasn't her problem.

When Lydia had found out about her new position and the event, she had tried to secure Lacey an invitation much to Ria's amusement. The answer had been a firm no. As the daughter of a Baron, Lacey didn't meet the requirements of rank or income that dictated who would be invited to the event.

Lady Marie looked up from her own correspondence and smiled at Ria, "You're finished? My, you are efficient."

Ria heard Andres sniff from across the room, "She's done nothing but write for the past three days."

She had looked forward to, and enjoyed, seeing him every day but neither of them had considered that his grandmother would also be there. Shooting him an amused glance, Ria sat back from the coffee table she had been using as a writing desk to stretch. Andres had tried to convince her to use part of his desk, but there hadn't been enough room for the spread of papers. He'd ended up having to content himself with walking by her and whispering amusing things in her ear when his grandmother wasn't looking. Lady Marie looked unconcerned as she stood to take the finished invitations.

The butler tapped on the open door, and said, "The seamstress is here for Miss Victoria."

"Oh good," Lady Marie replied, "Show her to the parlor."

Lady Marie and Ria went to meet the seamstress in the other room with Andres following behind. There was a flurry of activity in the parlor as the lady and her two assistants set up samples of cloth, ribbons and trimmings, and books with detailed drawings of all the different dresses which were in style.

Walking over to them, Ria flipped through the pages admiring them more for the artistry than the actual clothes being displayed. Someone had spent a lot of time on all the details in the line sketches, making sure that the lace and patterns were correct and the garments were so tempting you wanted to pull them off the page and wear them.

Andres moved behind her, bumping her shoulder with his chest. He reached over her arm and pointed to one of the dresses on the page.

"I believe this one would suit you quite well."

Ria looked at the dress he was pointing at, then down to her ample cleavage, and said, "I'm not sure that would be... modest enough."

"Perhaps you're right," he whispered a hair's breadth away from her ear, causing her to shiver as his words tickled her. Flushing, she elbowed him in the stomach, receiving a chuckle in response.

Andres watched as the seamstress' helper led Ria to a pedestal and helped her to stand on it. The assistant whipped out a measuring tape and moved around Ria's body as she stood with her arms out. When she didn't blink, but rather stared at one spot on the wall, he knew she must be daydreaming. When she was sitting in the library among the bookshelves, he would watch her, wondering what she was thinking about when that wistful expression crossed her face.

Fingering a cloth sample, admiring the softness of the fabric, he wondered how it would feel against her soft skin. He looked over at her again thinking of how the soft green color would match her eyes perfectly. Andres was eager to see her in the new dresses. He had become tired of seeing the contemptuous looks and hearing the snide whispers about her from the corners of the salons and ballrooms. She was too amazing, too good of a person, to have to suffer Society's cattiness.

Walking over to Ria as the assistant finished taking her measurements, Andres placed the square of cloth over one of her shoulders, making sure he still had a good view of her delicious bosom.

"I think this is a good color for you," he said, grinning up at her as she turned red again. Her blushing was adorable.

A pincer clamped down on his ear, and he let out a gasp of pain as his grandmother dragged him to the door. "In public, you will behave," she hissed at him before shoving him through the portal.

He winked at Ria who rolled her eyes in return just before his grandmother slammed the door in his face. He laughed heartily as he went back to his work.

Andres waited with Vince, who had arrived back in town the previous week, in the parlor at his grandmother's house. She had insisted that Ria come there to get dressed for the last ball of the season as one of her new gowns had arrived in time for the event.

Pacing back and forth with impatience, Andres walked to the stairs and called up, "Ladies, we are already fashionably late!"

"I am never late. Everyone else is early," his grandmother replied coming down the stairs.

Andres chuckled, "That is only true at your own events, Grandmother." He kissed her on both cheeks as she reached him before looking up the stairs for Ria.

He almost gasped in surprise and had to control his features when he saw her. She was a vision of loveliness in the new dress which, he was very pleased to see, was cut from the green fabric he had picked out. With her golden hair decorated with green ribbons and piled artfully on top of her head, straightened back and shoulders, and confidence gleaming from her eyes, she looked as regal as a duchess. He was about to hold a hand out to help her down the last few stairs when Vince pushed him out of the way.

"A more beautiful sight I have never seen," Vince said, giving her a courtly bow and holding his hand out to her. Ria groaned but took his hand and continued down the stairs. When she reached the bottom, Vince tucked her hand into the crook of his arm and escorted her to the door, shooting a smug look over his shoulder at Andres who glowered back. Taking his grandmother's hand, Andres escorted her to the waiting carriage.

After escorting the women through the greeting line, the men disappeared leaving Ria alone with the Grand Duchess. Lady Marie left Ria near the dance floor when she saw a few of her friends she wished to speak with. Ria was used to being alone and didn't mind in the slightest, enjoying the sight of the dancing couples.

"Victoria," Lydia said from behind her, startling her slightly, "I would like to introduce Sir Garvey to you. He lives close to your uncle's estate."

Ria tried not to grimace. The same age as her father and uncle, she had met the gentleman previously when he visited Thornfield to see her father. He brought his daughters, who were slightly younger than her, with him when he came to the estate. He was balding and always smelled of tobacco and whiskey with a rancid undertone of a strong body odor. There was something about the way he leered at her that made her uncomfortable. She wondered why Lydia looked like the cat who'd gotten the canary earlier that evening before she'd left for the Duchess's house, she must have known Sir Garvey was in town.

Taking her hand, he bowed over it and said, "May I have the pleasure of the next dance?"

"Of course," she replied even though she would rather be anywhere else. It would be considered rude to deny him a dance. He chatted with Lydia for a moment about the weather in London and then, as the next set started, took Ria's hand and led her to the floor. She was rather proud of the neutral face she was able to maintain, especially since she to breathe through the offensive smell emanating from him.

"Is Lady Garvey in town? I'd like to pay my respects to her." She had no intention of seeking out Lady Garvey as the woman was a harpy of the first order.

"Sadly, my wife passed several years ago. No, I came to London with your brother," Sir Garvey said, surprising her.

"I'm sorry for your loss. I hadn't heard my brother was in town, he never called."

"Yes, well, we've been spending most of our time between the clubs and halls. His time has been consumed with other pursuits," he replied when they came close enough together that they could speak again.

She looked at him out of the corner of her eye. Her brother had always been a gambler, but he never excelled at the pursuit. She wondered how much he lost this time. It was her family's hope that if he married and had responsibilities in the country, he would quit his bachelor lifestyle and help her father as the steward of her uncle's estate. Sighing inwardly, she realized that it must not have helped.

"Don't worry," Sir Garvey said, not even trying to hide the fact he was staring at her chest. "I won't let him lose too much."

"I thank you, Sir," she replied, pursing her lips and hoping the dance would be over soon. After he led her off the floor, she would seek out Lady Marie and stay by her side. Hopefully, the other woman would be able to make this man leave her alone. She caught Andres' eye as Garvey spun her into a twirl and tried to give him a subtle yet meaningful look.

Andres watched as some country nobody twirled his Ria around the dance floor and felt an uncomfortable sensation in his chest. He had no right to think of her that way. About to turn away and rejoin the other gentlemen at the card tables, he noticed the look on her face. She seemed, to him, upset though he doubted anyone else would be able to read the expression.

As her partner walked her off of the floor, he joined them and smiled, "Grandmother has been looking for you. Please allow me to escort you to her."

"Thank you for the dance, Sir Garvey," she said to her partner, trying to pull her hand from his grasp.

He brought it to his lips and placed a kiss across her gloved knuckles, lingering longer than was proper. "The pleasure was all mine, Miss Victoria. I look forward to seeing you again before we leave London."

Andres growled at the man who looked up at him with narrowed eyes but said nothing. He took his leave of them, walking into the card room. If the cad were still here after dinner, he would have a nice long chat with him.

"What did he want?" he asked Ria, tucking her hand into the crook of his arm and leading her towards his grandmother.

"One cannot even begin to guess," she replied, frowning, "But I have a feeling it has something to do with my brother. Nothing that Sir Garvey is involved with ever turns out well."

Andres narrowed his eyes in the direction the man had taken but said nothing. He would have to look into the matter. If anyone was out for Ria or her family, they would have to deal with him first. He would guarantee that the experience wouldn't be pleasant.

Ria tried to ignore the stares of the ton as she made her way with Andres back to his grandmother's side. She knew there would be no gossiping about them, Lady Marie would make sure of it. No one wanted to offend the Duchess or risk being socially snubbed by her.

"Ah, Andres, you've found her. Good," Lady Marie said as they approached her. "I'm having a lovely chat with my friends here, and it's almost time for dinner. Why don't you take Victoria for a turn on the dance floor before everyone leaves for the meal?"

Ria tried rather unsuccessfully not to smile. Lady Marie had just set them up for the dinner dance which meant that they would spend the rest of the evening together. Andres took her hand and bowed over it, "May I have the next dance?"

"It would be my pleasure, Your Grace," she said, curtsying to him.

He stood and led her to the dance floor, keeping a stoic look on his face, though she could see the glimmer of amusement in his eyes. She felt the rest of the evening would be very pleasant, perhaps the best she had ever experienced.

Chapter 7

*L*ooking around the ballroom at Andres' home, Ria though over the whirlwind of activity the past weeks had been. Within days of the last ball of the Season, she and Lady Marie had delivered all the invitations for the winter festival at Alnwick Castle. They had already received several acceptance letters.

Due to weather conditions, they expected guests to arrive around the third week of November for the December first start. Their party would need to leave in the last week of October, weather permitting, to arrive with enough time to make their final preparations and make sure the house was in order for their guests. Due to Lady Marie's limited ability to travel and the stops they would require to change horses and rest, they estimated it would take between eight and ten days to arrive in Alnwick. She barely had four weeks to prepare for the trip before they left.

Ria was disappointed that her brother had never stopped to call upon her in the weeks he had been in London. Sir Garvey had, much to her displeasure, called several times. Luckily, as she spent so much of her time in the company of Lady Marie, she had only been at home twice when he came. He had attempted to visit once at the Duchess' home but was promptly turned away. During his last unavoidable visit, Sir Garvey informed her that he and her brother would return to the country within the week. She was glad he was gone; the man made her skin crawl.

Today was their last dance lesson. It had taken several weeks to find a dance master that was free, but somehow Andres had managed to procure the best in the city. The man was an insufferable taskmaster, but she had to admit, she had improved exponentially. A violinist set up his instrument in the corner to lend music to the steps.

Andres walked up to her and smiled, "You look deep in thought today."

"More likely exhausted. Your grandmother has been running me ragged," she said with a half-smile, "I have no idea how she has so much energy." Lady Marie had been toting her to party after party, introducing her to all the other high-ranking ladies in Society and teaching her everything Society would expect a duchess to know. She paid close attention to the lessons though she doubted she would ever need the information.

"She is a feisty one," he replied, laughing.

"Yes, that's what Grandfather said," she winked at him, eliciting further merriment.

Taking her hand, Andres led her into position near the dance master. He placed his hand on her back, taking her other one in a soft grasp. His hands were warm against her, and she could smell the aftershave he wore, a spicy scent of sandalwood and cloves. Closing her eyes for a moment, she enjoyed the stolen closeness before the dance master adjusted the way they were standing.

Several of the steps they had adjusted, being too ridiculous for Andres to even consider performing, and had almost invented their own dance. They had been taking the lessons for over eight weeks, and she would miss being held by him like this. Perhaps she could convince him to practice with her after they reached Alnwick. She laughed lightly to herself while considering the ways she could persuade him.

"What's so amusing?" he asked as she opened her eyes.

"Nothing." The music started, and he led her into the opening steps of the waltz, watching her face as they danced.

"You've improved," he said. As a naturally coordinated dancer, he had outpaced her during the lessons.

"If you mean I haven't stepped on your foot yet, then yes, I have!" He laughed shaking his head while the dance master clapped his hands to stop them and adjusted her steps. She flashed Andres a wide-eyed glance as they started again.

It was almost the end of the lesson, and she couldn't help but look down at her feet. When she was nervous about making the correct steps, she would keep glancing down as if that would help her move correctly. Andres pulled in the hand that was holding hers and placed his finger gently under her chin, tilting her head up.

"Feel the music," he whispered, "Feel how it moves through your body. Feel the rhythm and follow my lead. Trust in me, I won't let you fall." He was gazing solemnly into her eyes, and her heart beat faster. As they moved, he pulled her closer until there was hardly any gap between them. The air grew thick as butterflies formed in her stomach. It was an odd but pleasurable feeling.

They flowed around the dance floor with one another, and Ria saw nothing but him. His eyes searched her face, lingering on her lips as his parted. The hairs on the back of her neck stood on end as she realized that if he came any closer, his lips would be upon hers. She swallowed but didn't look away, tilting her head higher.

The dance master cleared his throat next to them, breaking the spell. "That was fantastic, though you were standing too close to each other. Your technique has improved measuredly. All in all, I believe you will be a success."

Ria stood there and blinked at him dumbly for a moment while trying to gather her thoughts. A footman near the door interrupted them and called Andres away for a visitor. He gazed at her, his face unreadable, before excusing himself to attend to his business. Curtsying to the dance master, Ria followed him out to rejoin Lady Marie in the drawing room.

Two days after the last dance lesson, Ria sat in the drawing room of her home reading. She hadn't seen Andres yesterday when she stopped by to exchange books, the butler telling her he'd been at the docks all day dealing with business regarding his trade ships. Lady Marie had told her to stay home for the day, wanting to rest before the flurry of packing and preparing started. This suited Ria just fine, she was looking forward to some alone time.

Lydia flounced into the room, and Ria groaned inwardly, trying to ignore her. Sitting in the chair across from her, Lydia smiled and said, "I have wonderful news! Your cousin and I have found out we are expecting." She was beaming.

"Congratulations," Ria replied, raising her eyebrows.

"The baby is due in February. My parents will come to stay with us so they can chaperone Lacey."

"All right," Ria drew the words out until it became more of a question.

"They will be staying in the room you currently occupy."

Ria frowned, her eyebrows drawing together as Lydia continued, "Your mother has written a note and is requesting that you come home for the remainder of the winter. I sent a reply with Sir Garvey stating that you will arrive shortly after your duties with Lady Marie are over. Of course, you won't have a home here any longer, so this is for the best."

"Does Grandfather know about this?" anger tinged Ria's voice when she responded.

"He does. He's ecstatic to hear he will have a great-grandchild."

"He won't let you put me out," she replied.

Lydia gave her a smug smile, "Yes, well, he's old. Who knows how much time he has left."

"You are an absolute bitch," Ria said, standing up to leave the room.

Jumping to her feet, Lydia screamed, "How dare you!" She laughed and then added, "Not that I care what you think of me."

Turning at the doorway, Ria rose her chin and said, "You should care. I've spent the last few months meeting every high-ranking lady in society. I will make sure you and your little twit of a sister become social outcasts. You will not set foot in another drawing room by the time I am done. When you pass people on the streets, they will look at you with disdain." Lydia's mouth dropped open with a look of horror as Ria left the room.

Later that night, when sitting with her grandfather playing chess, Ria watched him. Lydia had been working all day to suck up to him. She had insisted on bringing him his food and wine as well as sitting next to him at dinner. She watched him the whole time, cajoling him to eat more when he would have finished, saying he needed to keep up his strength for when his new great-grandchild arrived. For his part, he took it in stride, trying not to upset her.

Ria moved a piece on the board, saving her Queen from one of his Bishops, and said, "Lydia says I'm not to come back from Thornbridge as there won't be any room for me here."

"Lydia doesn't know what she speaks of. I told her that her parents might stay here while they found a townhouse of their own," he said, glaring at the door. "It's one thing to let her sister stay here while she has her Season, but I have no interest in housing their entire clan." He rubbed his stomach and winced.

"What's wrong?"

"I don't think dinner agreed with me. I've been having issues over the past few weeks with rich foods and wine," he sighed, "Perhaps it's time to start eating the blander foods the cook keeps trying to feed me."

"I don't envy you that struggle," Ria said, wincing as he took her Queen anyhow.

She frowned at the board and took one of his castles, trying to set a trap for his Queen. Tapping her fingers on the arm of the chair, she asked, "I will be able to come back to London in the spring?"

"You wouldn't be concerned about a certain young man, would you?" he asked nonchalantly. Her gaze flew up to his face, noting the conspiratorial smile playing across his features.

"Why would you ask something like that?"

"You forget," he laughed, "I talk to the Duchess. I believe she has plans for the two of you."

She looked down, trying not to let tears fill her eyes, and replied, "He is far out of my league. I don't think all the planning in the world will change that."

"We'll see," he grunted in reply, putting her into checkmate. Narrowing her eyes at the board, she tried to fathom how he had managed to beat her so easily.

"You're distracted," he said, noting her examination of the pieces. She sighed, sitting back in the chair. They were generally evenly matched, but tonight he had managed to beat her several times in a row. Perhaps she was distracted with Andres and with what Lydia had told her.

"Come to Alnwick with us," she said to him, "I fear I will miss you too much if you stay here."

He laughed and replied, "No, that sort of travel is for the young and those who can't avoid it. I will see you in the spring when you return to London."

"Don't worry, Sweet pea." He stood and took her hand, drawing her up into a hug. "Everything will work out in the end, you'll see." He rubbed his scratchy whiskers in her hair holding her tightly for a moment longer. "Now go to bed. It's long past time we retired."

"I'll see you tomorrow Grandpapa. I love you," she said, smiling and, standing on her tiptoes, placed a kiss on his cheek.

"But I love you most of all," he replied.

When the housekeeper came to wake her the next morning, tears streaming from her eyes, Ria knew something was terribly wrong. The housekeeper informed her that her grandfather had passed away in the night.

Ria sat in numb silence to one side of the parlor where her grandfather's body was laid for his wake. The previous day had been a long and grueling exercise in her ability to push her feelings aside and take care of business. She'd written letters to her grandfather's closest friends informing them of his passing. After finishing the letters for those close by, she'd written to her mother and her uncle, her grandfather's younger son, to let them know their father had passed. She'd met with the doctor to verify her grandfather's passing and then contacted the funeral furnisher.

After writing the announcement of death for the morning paper and setting viewing hours, she'd been too exhausted and drained to do more than pick at her dinner. Thankfully, everything else was to be handled by the people they'd hired to arrange the funeral and subsequent transport of her grandfather's remains to their family crypt at Amberly Hall.

Lydia had acted like the queen of the castle, ordering everyone around more than usual. Without Grandfather's presence to counteract her orders, the servants had to obey. Her attitude, mixed with their resentment, cast a dark shadow over the house.

She looked up and watched Lady Marie greet guests and direct them away from her when possible. If another person came up to her and said they were sorry for her loss, she might lose her mind. Most people seemed to understand with one look at her face and turned the other way. The furnisher had worked fast to provide her grandfather with a proper viewing. The funeral would be the next day, and then, after the attendants sealed the coffin, her grandfather would be on his way home to be interred next to her grandmother.

Sniffing lightly to clear her face, she took a deep breath to brace herself and stood up to join Lady Marie and her cousin in the procession of guests. She almost made it to them without crying until she saw Andres standing next to his grandmother, talking softly to her with his head bent. When he looked up and saw her, his eyes meeting hers, she lost her composure again. Tears streamed down her face, and her upper lip quivered as he came over to her.

Andres saw Ria standing behind his grandmother, and his heart broke. She looked so small and lost, her eyes red and puffy from crying and lack of sleep. He couldn't help himself, he walked over to her and drew her into his embrace, holding her tightly. The moment he touched her, she sobbed quietly into his shoulder, holding onto him as tightly as he held her. Holding the back of her head with one hand, he whispered nondescript but soothing words to her.

The other guests stared at him wide-eyed, his daring them to say something. No one said a word about what would otherwise cause a scandal but rather went on with their business, saying their goodbyes before leaving to finish their day.

Eventually, Ria had cried herself out again, and he released her. He was worried at the paleness of her skin and the blank look in her eyes. Looking to his grandmother for help, he raised his eyebrows in silent question.

His grandmother walked over, rubbed her back softly, and murmured something in her ear. She seemed to consider for a moment before nodding. Motioning to a footman, she handed Ria over to him with a few whispered words, and he led her away.

When his grandmother rejoined him, he asked her, "What did you tell her?"

"I may be a horrible person, but…" she sighed, "I told her that her grandfather wouldn't want to see her become sick from mourning him and that she should lie down. I told her I would stay until the wake was over, it shouldn't be much longer."

Her lips trembled slightly as she said, "It's time I say my own goodbyes." She walked sedately over to the coffin and placed her hands on the edge. He saw her whispering softly.

While she and Ria's family were distracted, he walked from the room and found the butler overseeing the household. Pulling the man aside, he smiled, holding a folded ten-pound note in his hand.

"I believe there is a certain chess set that belonged to the late Earl. One he and his granddaughter would play with nightly," he said in a soft undertone to the man.

The butler looked over his shoulder and, seeing that no one was watching them, replied, "There is."

"Do you believe anyone in the family would miss it?"

"Only the young miss."

"Perfect," he said, slipping the note into the other man's hand. "If it were to happen to find its way into my carriage, I would be most obliged. There will, of course, be equal compensation when the task is finished."

The butler looked as if he were about to refuse but Lydia chose that moment to start screeching at one of the maids. He nodded instead.

Andres and his grandmother left together shortly thereafter once the rest of the guests had taken their leave. On his way out, he slipped another ten-pound note into the butler's hand when the man gave him a slight nod.

The funeral had been a painful affair, but it had truly made Ria realize how many other people loved her grandfather. People he had touched across all walks of life stood to give their final goodbyes and remembrances. She sat between Christian and one of her other cousins who happened to be in London. Neither of them spoke, but she knew they suffered his loss as well. All too soon, the service was over, and the coffin nailed shut, the cart carrying her grandfather's remains rolling down the street towards home.

Andres and Lady Marie had offered to take her home when Lydia made a huge fuss, insisting on leaving as soon as possible. Much to their surprise, Christian had asked if he could wait with them until their grandfather was out of sight.

Sitting in the carriage in front of their townhouse, no one made a move to leave the small but comforting space.

"We should go in," Christian sighed.

"You're the Earl of Amberly now," Ria said softly, looking up at him.

His eyes were full of sadness, but he took a deep breath, "A title I could have done without for a few more years." He looked out the window at the front door as if he would rather be anywhere else.

They disembarked from the carriage and walked up the front steps, entering the townhouse together. There was a flurry of activity moving from the upstairs to the back of the house, and Ria noticed the trunks piled up at the foot of the stairs.

"What's going on here?" Christian asked one of the servants.

Lydia came around the corner, her mourning dress gone and replaced with one of her regular day dresses, and gave them a smug smile, "Victoria is moving out, and we are cleaning out our new suite. We will have to completely remodel the whole room, of course, it's filled with stuffy furniture and old man smell."

Lady Marie gasped and, if Andres hadn't stepped in front of her at just that second, would have attacked Lydia.

Christian was fuming, "Victoria isn't going anywhere. My grandfather's things aren't going anywhere. His body isn't even in its final resting place, have you no respect?"

"Yes, she is. And yes, they are. I am the Countess now, this is my house," Lydia replied in a tone that ended the conversation, ignoring his question. She left the front room with her head held high.

The four of them stood there in shocked silence, staring at the hallway she had disappeared down. Christian's shoulders slumped in defeat.

"I will have Grandfather's things sent to Amberly," he said, "At least then the family can go through them at their leisure." He turned to Victoria, cupping her face with his hand, "I'm sorry Ria."

Andres stepped forward, "We will take care of her. She will move in with Grandmother. She is her companion, she should live with her anyhow."

Christian nodded and looked back down at her, "Find happiness Ria. Marry someone you love if you are able," he looked down the hall where Lydia had disappeared, "otherwise, life is miserable." He dropped his hand and then left in the opposite direction.

Andres waved down the butler who had been standing silently off to the side, watching the scene without comment, "Please have Miss Victoria's things delivered to my townhouse."

"Yes, Your Grace," he replied bowlng.

Pacing around her new bedroom, Ria sighed. She owed Andres an apology, and she hated to apologize. When they had arrived at his townhouse earlier that afternoon, she had accused him of taking her in like a stray puppy. She had told him she didn't want his pity and would find her own accommodations not considering she had no other relations in the city with whom to stay.

Andres, for his part, had snapped back angrily that he didn't pity her. He had said that, as his grandmother's companion, if anything he had been lenient in letting her continue to stay with her grandfather rather than moving in with Lady Marie.

The Duchess broke into the middle of their argument to announce that she was going to her room to rest as it had been a long and stressful last few days for everyone, putting much emphasis on the last words. It was as if a bubble had burst and the tension had left the room. Andres had put an arm around her shoulders and led her to one of the maids, asking the girl to escort her to the room next to his grandmother. She had looked up at him then and saw a softness in his gaze she hadn't noticed before.

The girl had led her to a beautiful room decorated in light blue and white striped silk. There were several windows that added natural light to the room and a cold fireplace in one corner. Plush furs on the floor lent softness over the dark hardwood floors. The room was delightful, but at the time the only thing Ria had her eye on was the large four-poster bed against the far wall.

She'd curled up in the middle and had a good long cry about all the things that had changed in her life until she'd fallen asleep. When her new maid woke her several hours later, she'd felt like a new person.

The maid helped her to dress for dinner in a new black gown she hadn't seen before, but fit her perfectly, and she realized that either Andres or Lady Marie had ordered it for her mourning. That had made her feel even worse about their earlier argument.

Steeling her nerve to face Andres, Ria made her way to the library before dinner. She found him working at his desk when she arrived, and she knocked lightly on the door.

Looking up and, seeing her, he frowned, "Why are you knocking?"

"What?" she asked, taken aback.

"You never knock. You generally just come in," he replied, grinning.

She glared at him for a moment and then walked into the room. "I didn't know if you were upset with me."

Sighing, he sat back in his chair, and said, "We wouldn't be human if we didn't argue now and then."

She smiled at him in return, "Regardless, I'm sorry for my words earlier. Thank you for your hospitality."

"I wasn't exaggerating when I said you should be staying with Grandmother."

She stuck her tongue out at him while walking to the couch in front of the fire. She stopped, frozen in place when she saw her grandfather's chess set where his had previously been. Taking a sharp breath, she tried not to start crying again as she walked over to it. Her shaking hand hovered over the pieces before selecting the black king, running her thumb over the carving with affection.

"How?" she asked, turning to Andres.

"I may have taken the liberty of appropriating it during the wake."

She held the piece as if it were a valuable treasure. "Thank you. Truly," she smiled at him, "I thought this was lost to me. I tried to enter Grandfather's chambers before the funeral, but the doors were locked. Grandfather never locked the doors, not once. I think that is the moment I knew things were never going to be the same."

"I have something for you as well," Lady Marie said from the doorway, startling her. Ria placed the king back in his spot and turned to her. Two servants carried a large chest into the room behind her and placed it next to the coffee table. Sitting in one of the armchairs, she gestured for Ria to open it.

Ria knelt in front of the chest, questions in her eyes, as she undid the clasp. Andres came to join them, interested in what his grandmother could have brought. When the lid opened, she cried out, covering her mouth with her hand. With the other, she reached gingerly into the chest and withdrew a music box that had been carefully wrapped in soft cloth. She opened it, winding the sound box, and let it play. A soft song twinkled from the item, stopping after a minute.

"This was my grandmother's," she said, enraptured with the little box, "it went missing several months ago. Lydia was furious. She thought the servants had stolen it, but Grandfather refused to listen to her. How?" She looked at Lady Marie with puzzlement written across her face.

"When your grandfather realized who the woman your cousin married was, he brought me the things he knew you held dear to your heart for safe keeping. He wanted to guarantee you would receive them upon his death though I'm sure he didn't think it would be so soon."

Ria pulled more items out of the chest. There was a lace scarf her grandmother had worn almost every day, two small dolls which she had loved to play with as a child, several pieces of her grandmother's jewelry she had favored, and many more items. Looking through them was like walking through her memories. She still missed her grandmother but, with time, the pain of her loss had lessened. She knew that, with these reminders, her grandfather was telling her with time, the pain of his passing would lessen as well, leaving behind fond memories.

Chapter 8

hat's it!" Lady Marie growled, "All of you, get out of this carriage. If you are going to act like children, you can travel like children!"

Ria struggled to contain her laughter while Lady Marie hit Vince with her cane. Turning to her, Lady Marie pointed a finger, "You too!"

"Me? I didn't do anything!" Ria started laughing as Lady Marie hit the top of the carriage to alert the driver and stop it. When it came to a full halt, Vince jumped out the door followed by Andres who turned to lift Ria down instead of pulling the steps out. He pulled her out of the way, his hands warm around her waist, as he avoided being hit with the closing door.

Walking over to Vince, Ria slugged him in the shoulder, laughing, and said, "This is all your fault! I told you to leave me alone."

"I just figured we could use some fresh air, it was all part of my master plan," he replied.

She rolled her eyes as Andres flagged down the footman in charge of the riding mounts. She lifted the hood on the new cloak he had given her for her birthday the week before to cover her head from the chill of the afternoon. It was a gorgeous pure white wool lined with deep amethyst silk, and it was incredibly warm. She'd hesitated to accept it, but he'd said the weather would be too cold for the patched and fraying cloak she owned and she'd had to agree with him.

Perhaps one of her favorite new wardrobe items was a riding habit Andres ordered from Paris. Crafted from dark blue wool, the outfit was perfectly tailored for her form. The best part about it, in her opinion, was the skirt which split in the middle so she could ride astride rather than sidesaddle. When she'd asked him about it, he said he was more concerned with her safety than what the ton biddies would say. Two grooms led their horses to them, handing one off to Vince who mounted with little effort and rode over.

"Tell Grandmother we are going to ride ahead to the inn. If she's going to make us sit out here in the cold, at least we can reach the warmth sooner," Andres told his brother grinning. Vince rode ahead to inform the Duchess of their plans.

Turning back to her, Andres held her saddle as she placed her left foot in the stirrup. "Do you need help?" he asked her.

"Probably," she replied, grimacing over her shoulder. Concentrating on the horse, she readied herself to mount. Andres laughed and placed his hand on her bum, pushing her onto the horse as she pulled herself up. Before letting go, he squeezed and winked at her as she twirled in surprise. Ria narrowed her eyes at him but said nothing as she adjusted her clothing around the horse. When she was prepared, she spurred her horse into a gallop, laughing as she rode past Vince and the rest of the party. She didn't make it far before Andres overtook her, his coal black Arab stallion barely making an effort. The horse seemed glad to run, and her smaller mare didn't seem to mind following after him.

"Me too, girl," she whispered to her, watching Andres's back move expertly with his horse.

After a few minutes at a gallop, always making sure that Ria was close to him without looking back, he slowed his horse to a trot and let her come up beside him. They were finally alone again for the first time in months without his brother or grandmother there to bother them.

He looked covertly at her and saw her face flushed from cold, her eyes sparkling, and a wide smile across her face. It made him smile to see her happy after weeks of sadness.

"You seem to be enjoying yourself," he said, smiling at her.

"I haven't had this much fun since I was a little girl and escaping the groom," she laughed. "I used to pretend that I lived in a fairytale castle, in the highest tower, and I would escape by taking the secret tunnels from my rooms. I would hie to the stables and steal the fastest mount to race across the countryside."

"Secret tunnels?"

"Ah," she grinned at him, "the servants' passages. The groom always had my mount saddled and ready to go, and I would ride like the wind. Truth be told, the groom was never far behind, and I think he pretended he couldn't keep up with me. Silver is a beautiful dappled grey pony. She still lives at Thornbridge, and I ride her every chance I get. I've always loved adventure." She paused, reminiscing, then turned to him and said, "What about you? What was your childhood like?"

"I don't remember much of it before I was sent to Eton," he replied. "I remember always being expected to act calm and composed. I was never allowed to run free; I suppose it was because of the duties I would one day inherit. Vince had much more freedom than I did, you can tell by his personality he wasn't whipped nearly enough as a child." Ria's laugh never failed to lighten his mood.

"I missed seeing your smile," he said, his eyes soft as he watched her.

She looked at him, cocking her head slightly to the side, before looking down at her hands on the reins. The smile didn't leave her face, but she answered in a subdued tone, "I'll admit it's been a hard few weeks, but I've never been the wailing in grief sort."

Looking past him into the forest, she continued, "Although I do grieve sometimes, late at night when I'm alone, I know that Grandfather wouldn't have wanted me to be sad. He would have told me 'Buck up sweet pea! There's a lot of life left out there to live!'."

Andres laughed, "I can imagine him saying that. I believe my grandfather actually said the same phrase to me once or twice. Although looking back, I'm almost certain he didn't use the expression in the same tone."

"They were best friends since Eton. I'm sure they had many stories about one another."

Andres heard a twig snap in the forest behind her, and his eyes flew towards the sound, searching the trees. Ria quieted at once, searching the trees as well. A flash of tan stood out against the background for a moment, not quite matching its surroundings.

"Did you see that?" Ria said over her shoulder, her voice low.

"We're too close to Nottingham for bandits. They wouldn't attack this close to the city on royal roads."

Andres saw nothing else from her side of the road, but just as he was about to relax, another twig snapped from the other side. He moved his hand under his coat to the handle of his pistol. It was loaded and primed, just needing to be cocked before it could be fired. He didn't like to take chances on the road and cursed his folly when he realized how far away from the main party they were. Glancing at Ria, he noticed pursed lips. She made no sound as they rode while trying to be less of a distraction.

He turned in his saddle when he heard the horses galloping behind him while automatically drawing his pistol. Ria gasped slightly, but he relaxed and put the gun away, not turning his horse when he saw it was Vince and three of their footmen riding towards them.

Frowning, Vince rode up next to him, and said, "What was that about?"

"We thought we saw something or someone in the woods," he replied, nodding to the other side of Ria.

Vince narrowed his eyes and turned to one of the footmen. "Ride back to the main party, tell them to stay vigilant. We will ride ahead and inform the city watch to send out a patrol." The man turned and rode back towards the main party with haste.

Spurring their horses into a fast trot, Ria turned to him, and said, "You aren't worried about your grandmother?"

"No," he smiled, "the main party is heavily armed. If there are bandits, they would be hard-pressed to rob them." He caught Vince's eye, motioning for the other man to flank Ria between them. Her safety was of utmost importance on the journey. They didn't hear any other noises or see any other oddities in the forest once the others joined them.

"Good night, my dears, I'm off to bed," Lady Marie told the room of young people as she stood up. She kissed Ria on the forehead and then kissed each of her grandsons on the cheek before retiring to the room she and Ria would share.

Upon arriving at the hotel earlier that day, they joined two of Andres' friends, Dimitri and Lucio, in a private three-room suite they had rented. The men were the same two she had seen with him the first night she had met him in the library. They were both incredibly good-looking men. She mused upon the fact that all of his close friends were brilliant, talented, and very wealthy.

Lucio, Italian by birth, was tall with light brown hair that hung around his face in long strands. He had the aquiline nose of his ancestors that drew the eyes to the most amazing blue-green eyes she'd ever seen. She couldn't decide if he or Dimitri was more attractive.

Dimitri, a resident of Greece, had features that were softer but no less alluring with slightly darker and shorter hair, hazel eyes, and soft lips. Both men towered over her, neither being under six feet tall. Still, though, she felt that neither of them held a candle to Andres. Perhaps she was partial to him and his personality though.

They currently occupied a table in the corner of the room playing a game of cribbage for stakes and drinking wine from the stock Lucio brought from his family's vineyards. From what Ria had noticed while reading on the couch, they were paying the difference in points to the winner. Andres was ahead of the other players, being skilled in reading his friends.

She'd waited until Lady Marie retired and then stood up to walk over to the men.

"Your game looks amusing," she said, smiling from behind Andres's shoulder.

"We play a lot of cribbage while traveling. It helps to pass the time," Andres replied, turning to her.

"Would you like to learn?" Vince piped up from across the table, "I'd be happy to show you how." He winked at her with a salacious grin.

She groaned and shuddered. "Oh God, literally anyone but you," she responded teasingly. All the men laughed as Vince pouted.

Andres scooted his chair back, pulling her into his lap, much to the amusement of the other two men. They shared a meaningful glance that Ria noticed but doubted Andres did. They had been cordial to her since their arrival, but neither of them had made much of an effort to talk to her. She couldn't decide if it was because she was a woman or an outsider.

"Do you play at all?" Andres asked her as Dimitri shuffled the cards.

"About as well as I play chess," she said, smiling at him over her shoulder.

Vince, perking up since he'd tried a game or two of chess against her, said, "I propose we play partners. We wouldn't want to give a disadvantage to an untried player after all."

"Ah, you partner with her, and the girl will lose for sure," Lucio teased him in a soft Italian accent.

"What will you stake for the bet, lovely?" Dimitri asked.

She could feel Andres tense under her, but before he could respond, she said, "It doesn't really matter, I don't intend to lose." She grinned cheekily as the men laughed in response. Dimitri dealt the cards and Vince made the first cut. They left the card facedown as everyone picked up their hands.

"I will cover her, naturally," Andres said, smiling over her shoulder. He wrapped his hands around her waist, enjoying her softness in his lap, while she looked over her cards. She'd received a decent deal of an ace, a six, two sevens, and an eight. He laid his nose on her shoulder, running his lips over the soft skin under them. She shivered and threw the ace into the crib.

"If that's the case, I propose we up the wager to two shillings a point," Lucio grinned, believing he would win back his losses off of her.

"Deal," Andres said, not giving the other man time to reconsider the wager.

"And you can't help her," Dimitri added.

Andres grinned into the back of her neck, "I wouldn't dream of it."

He took a deep breath, enjoying her scent, as Dimitri flipped the card on the top of the deck. She gave no outward reaction as she cut another seven. He grinned into her shoulder as Vince opened the board.

"Four."

Andres dug his fingers into the softness of her waist, brushing his thumb over the warm fabric of her dress.

Ria tilted her head slightly but said nothing as Lucio played a five next. "Nine," he counted off.

She narrowed her eyes at him, tapping her cards on the table as if waiting for the trap to fall. After studying Lucio for a few more moments, she played the six.

"Fifteen for two and a run of three for five points," she said, sitting back further into his embrace. Andres doubted that Dimitri had the seven for a run since three of them were already out of play. At most he would peg four points if he played a three. It was a safe play to make.

Dimitri, shrugging, played a jack and counted, "Twenty-five."

Vince grinned at him and played his six, giving them an extra two points for the round, and counted, "Thirty-one for two."

Lucio started the next round with the count, "Eight."

Running his lips over the nape of Ria's neck, barely touching the skin, he smiled at the gooseflesh that ran over her skin as he tickled the small hairs.

"Sixteen, a pair for two," Ria responded, playing her eight in turn. Vince pegged the points on the board.

"Twenty-six," Dimitri said, throwing down a queen.

"Twenty-nine," Vince followed with a three.

"Thirty," Lucio threw down an ace.

"Go," Ria told him, smiling as he took his team's first point. She glanced over her shoulder at Andres with a raised eyebrow, and he grinned in return.

Ria threw down one of her remaining sevens to start the next round of play, "Seven."

Dimitri added a king to the pile, "Seventeen."

Vince played his last card, a two, "Nineteen."

"Twenty-eight," Lucio counted, throwing his last card in, and added, "Leave the poor girl alone, Andres."

"Go," Ria said, giving them another point, and then played her last card, "Seven."

"Twelve and one for last card," Dimitri said throwing his last card in, taking their point. Andres glared at Lucio who shook his head in return.

They all laid their cards out in front of themselves, ready for the final count of the round. When Vince saw her cards, he laughed so hard he shook the table. Ria, grinning, wiggled excitedly in his lap to the point where he had to hold her tighter to stop her or he wouldn't be able to stand up from the table.

"I know, I doubt my pretty little head can count that high. It's so hard once you run out of fingers, after all. I might need your help," she grinned at Lucio.

He glowered at her while he took a sip of dark red wine, and turned to Vince, "Count."

"Fifteen two and a run of three is five," he said, pegging the five points.

"Fifteen two, fifteen four, and a run of three for seven," Lucio followed, taking his points on the board.

Ria sighed while looking down at her cards and he couldn't help but note the smile that spread across her face, "Let's see. Fifteen two, fifteen four, fifteen six, a triple run of three for fifteen, and three of a kind for twenty-one points. Did I miss any?"

Two sets of eyes glared at her as a very amused Vince added their points on the board. Andres tried his hardest to suppress his laughter, running his hands over her thighs under the table before reaching for his own glass of wine. She placed her hand over his hand that remained on her leg, holding it in place and tightening her grip, as Dimitri counted his hand and then the crib and took his teams points. Vince and Ria were well ahead of the others.

After several rounds, they finished the game with Ria and Vince leading by over twenty points, thanks to Ria's skill and a little luck with the flips.

"I thought you said *la bellezza* didn't know how to play," Lucio said to Andres, sitting back in his chair with a putout expression.

Andres narrowed his eyes, not sure if he liked his friends referring to her with any sort of endearment, and replied, "She said she plays about as well as she plays chess. She beats me three out of five games."

Ria sniffed, "More than."

Tickling her ribs until she laughed and moved slightly, Andres told his friend, "She does that, lets people think she doesn't know a game and then trounces them."

"Only people I like," she said, grinning over her shoulder at him. Their faces where scant centimeters apart and he saw something flash in her eyes before she looked away, picking up the new hand Vince had just dealt.

"Teams again?" she asked.

"Fine," Lucio replied, "but she needs to start drinking, or she'll take us for all we have."

Chapter 9

Ria woke the next morning to a maid opening the curtains in her room. The Duchess was absent when she looked around, and she didn't know when the other woman had left. Groaning, she rubbed her forehead as pain shot through her skull.

"What time is it?" she asked the maid.

"Around eleven in the morning," the other woman responded, moving to the wardrobe to select a dress for her.

"Are you sure?" she asked, shooting upright, then clutching her head again as the blood rushed into it. "I'm never drinking again."

The maid guffawed, "That's what everyone says the morning after imbibing, my dear. Lady Marie expects all of you down in the restaurant for a midday meal."

"I assume, if it's eleven, that we aren't leaving today?"

The maid nodded to the window. Sleet was pounding against the glass, the outside world grey and almost dark as night. "No one wants to travel in this."

Ria threw back the covers and stood. After steadying herself, she went to the washbasin and cleaned her face and hands in the steaming water the maid had just poured. The maid helped her dress in one of the warmer gowns and placed her slippers on the floor next to the bed so she could slip them on.

Once she finished dressing, she made her way to the outer suite. Taking a seat on the couch with her feet propped up on an ottoman, she awaited the others. A footman came over to her carrying a glass with an evil-looking concoction in it. The base had to be tomatoes, and it smelled worse than it looked. Scrunching her nose at the smell, she tried not to gag as she took it.

"Don't drink that," Andres said, coming out of a bedroom with Vince following behind him.

"Why not?"

"At best, it will make you throw up. At worst, well, it will still make you throw up," he chuckled, taking the glass from her and handing it back to the footman, shaking his head. The man left with the glass as Vince took an armchair.

Andres laid down on the couch and placed his head in her lap while groaning. She said nothing and ran her fingers through his hair, twirling his curls between them. Vince watched them with an odd expression but made no comment on their behavior.

"How much did we drink last night?" she asked Vince.

"Not enough to stop you from taking us for all we had," Lucio replied, coming out of the other bedroom. He raised an eyebrow at Andres but also made no comment.

"I vaguely remember telling you we didn't have to play for stakes after the third game," she responded.

He laughed and took the last armchair. "Dimitri will be out shortly. He needs to work on his tolerance," he said with an evil grin.

Andres groaned and turned his body towards the back of the couch, burying his face in her stomach. "Wake me up when he arrives," he said, his voice muffled by the fabric of her dress. He nuzzled her.

"Excuse me, sir," she laughed down at him but didn't stop playing with his hair. She had a difficult time ignoring the heat of his breath through the thin fabric of her dress. He chuckled, and she could see his grin, but he stopped.

Dimitri came out of the room looking for all the world like he'd had the best night's sleep of his life.

"Why is it," she asked, examining him, "that you look healthy and refreshed while the rest of us look like we've been drug through the streets."

"Whatever do you mean?" he replied, stealing a bun off a tray the footmen brought around.

"I keep telling him hangovers get worse after thirty," Andres said, looking over his shoulder, "He'll learn."

Dimitri shrugged, "I also drank that vile stuff the footman gave me."

They laughed as a footman came in to announce that Lady Marie was waiting for them downstairs. Andres stood, holding out his hand to assist her, and gave her his arm as they made their way to lunch.

"Lord Kentwood, what a pleasure to see you," Ria said, hoping the disdain in her voice didn't show, as they greeted Lady Marie's companions. "And your lovely sister as well." The last time she saw the Lord, he was chasing the skirts of a young widow down a hallway during a soiree.

Kentwood looked at her with a sneer, "Miss Sutton, I had heard you were traveling with the Duchess' party, but I didn't believe it."

The smile she gave him didn't touch her eyes. As she turned to take her seat, he leaned close to her ear and whispered, "Let me know when Northumberland has finished with you. I ordinarily wouldn't take his seconds, but there is a certain," he paused, leering down her dress, "robustness about you I find attractive."

Her eyes widened with anger, but before she could say anything, Vince stepped between them, placing his hand gently on her upper arm. His eyes were hard when he focused on the other man, "Kentwood, I believe my grandmother wishes to hear news of your travels." Kentwood gave him a half smile, his eyes lingering on Ria overlong before he went to take his seat.

Vince placed her in between himself and his brother. Kentwood's younger sister, Abigale, sat on the other side of Andres. Across the table from them, Lucio, Dimitri, Kentwood, and the Duchess took their places.

As the Duchess kept Kentwood occupied, Abigale carried on a lively conversation with Andres. Because she was Lacey's best friend, Abigale had a very similar demeanor. She simultaneously complemented Andres while slandering Ria. Although she tried not to pay attention to their conversation, she couldn't help but overhear how Abigale believed only those of noble birth should be allowed to attend the winter gathering.

While she spoke, Abigale kept touching Andres' arm and hand, letting hers linger before removing it to emphasize whatever she was saying. Ria tried to ignore them, but a weight in her chest kept her from enjoying the meal. While not wanting to be jealous of the girl, she couldn't deny that with their family's nobility and their social status, they were considered an excellent match. Instead of pushing around the food on her plate, her stomach deciding to rebel at the thought of eating the rich fare, she turned to Vince, Lucio, and Dimitri.

"I don't remember if I asked last night, but how do you two know Andres and Vince?" she asked them. She could feel Abigale's glare burning into her skin as she used the brother's first names rather than titles, but she didn't care.

Dimitri's gaze flicked over first her, then Andres, then Abigale, noticing the tension in the three of them. "I am the Admiral of his trade fleet, and Lucio's family owns a group of vineyards in the Italian countryside that Andres favors," he responded.

"That sounds fascinating," she replied, "Do you travel with the ships?"

"I do. This time of the year, I would be south of Spain where the temperatures are considerably more tolerable. However, Andres asked if I would attend this gathering he was hosting, so I agreed."

"What's it like, living on a ship and traveling the world? Have you been to the Americas? I've read about them, but I'd love to speak with someone who has a firsthand account."

Dimitri laughed and indulged her in conversation.

Andres half listened to the conversation Dimitri and Ria were having, trusting his friend to keep her amused while he considered Kentwood. He had seen the man lean down to speak with her and, noting her expression in response, wanted to know what vileness he was spreading. Vince had stepped between them before Andres could react and he trusted his brother to keep an eye on her. She was important to his family. His friends accepted her the night before, hesitantly at first, but warming to her after a few games were played and beverages imbibed.

While contemplating whether he should have a word with Kentwood, and trying to ignore how the man looked at Ria, Abigale tried to grab his attention. He had listened to her at first but quickly grew bored with the conversation. It was hard to hold his attention for long. Ria was the only woman who had managed so far. Even his past mistresses in London could only keep his attention for a few weeks. He wondered if it had anything to do with the mental connection he shared with Ria.

Perhaps his grandmother was correct, and it was time he took a wife. He hadn't realized how obsessed he had become with his work until Ria had entered his life to distract him. The path his life had taken since becoming the Duke of Northumberland wasn't healthy. His father had met an early end from overindulgence, having more interest in women and gambling than his duties to his family.

Andres had taken his responsibilities in the opposite direction. He built his family's lands and fortunes to twice what they had been when he inherited, and they continued to grow. Perhaps it was time he focused on the next generation. He would have to think about it in greater detail.

"Andres," Ria said, placing her hand on his arm, startling him from his reverie.

"Yes?" he replied, ignoring Abigale's sniff of disdain. He hadn't heard a word she'd spoken to him anyhow.

"Dimitri was telling me how you stole his home in Greece," she said, her eyes filled with laughter.

He sniffed and laughed, "Yes, he loves to tell that story though he never gets it quite right. It involves two pistols, a table, and a donkey. Here is what really happened."

Chapter 10

The last few days of travel had dragged on, and Ria was excited to arrive at Alnwick. While the carriage rolled into the bailey around the castle, she thought back over their journey. After a light supper the second night in Nottingham, the men, along with Kentwood, had left for the gaming hells. She had spent the rest of the night reading, a pastime she never minded, as Lady Marie worked on embroidery.

Roused early the next morning, she and the Duchess left in the carriage as the weather was more conducive to travel. After staying out until dawn broke the horizon, the men said they would take horses and catch up to them in the afternoon. Lady Abigale traveled with them as their paths were similar for another two days before she and her brother split off to visit a property outside the borders of Northumberland.

Abigale did her best to ignore Ria, chattering at the Duchess who, after a while, just stared at her. Unfortunately, as the lowest ranking member in the carriage, she was forced to ride backward. She had tried to read at first but quickly realized it would be impossible. They'd had to stop when her stomach protested, and she'd had to avail herself of the bushes on the side of the road, much to Abigale's amusement. She'd been unable to continue traveling in the carriage, the confined space and backward motion too uncomfortable to bare.

Instead, she'd rode with a footman ahead of the carriage. He'd been quiet at first, but soon she'd convinced him to open up and talk to her. She knew it was odd and against convention, but if she couldn't read or sleep, she needed something to amuse her during the long hours in the saddle. Telling her about the girl he was interested in back home, she gave him advice from the books she'd read.

They heard riders galloping from behind and stopped to wait as the men came into view. As soon as they rode up, the footman fell back to join the main group of travelers. Abigale joined them on horseback, making sure to ride next to Andres whenever he was available, dominating his attention. She sat a perfect seat on the sidesaddle, looking like a queen examining her army.

When Vince, Lucio, and Dimitri took turns flanking her, she realized they were keeping themselves as a barrier between her and Kentwood, who kept watching her. The man made lurid comments to her, as if she welcomed his advances, whenever he had the chance. She didn't like his attention and wished he would leave her alone, believing he didn't see her as a person, only as a conquest that would infuriate the other men. They would soon split from the party, she had reminded herself, to keep her spirits high.

Finally, they had arrived in York. After one more night of the Kentwood siblings company, they had parted ways much to the relief of their party. The last leg of their journey, once they were alone and free to be themselves, was far more relaxing and enjoyable.

Their carriage came rolling to a stop, breaking into her thoughts and she looked out the window at the imposing structure before her. She admired the sculptures sitting atop the ramparts and the impressive architecture of the castle.

A footman opened the door for them, folding down the stairs so they could descend. Lady Marie left the carriage followed by Ria, and the servants lined along the walkway before them, curtsied or bowed to them. Andres and the other men rode into the bailey and dismounted, handing their reins over to the grooms.

Vince stretched, yawning, and said, "I'm done for. I'm going to my rooms to rest while I can. Hunting tomorrow?"

"No," Andres sniffed, "I have things to take care of. Amuse yourselves however you see fit." He held his hand out to Ria, "I want to show you something." Curious, she took his hand and followed him down several winding hallways.

"I grew up here," he said, surprising her, "I have many favorite spots, places I would hide when I didn't want my nurse to find me. There is one in particular, however, that I believe you will enjoy."

Stopping in front of a set of double doors, he turned to her smiling, and said, "Cover your eyes."

She raised her eyebrow at him but did as he asked, laughing when she felt the air swirl in front her face when he waved a hand to see if she peeked. Satisfied, he opened the doors and took both of her hands, leading her through.

Moving behind her, he placed his hands on her waist and whispered into her ear, "Open your eyes."

Ria followed his direction and gasped in wonder as she looked around. They were standing in the midst of a library twice as large as the one in the townhouse. Light oak shelves held books of every size amongst them. Between the shelves, intricate carvings graced panels topped with scrolled arms, carrying the weight of the second floor. Small decorative lamps, unlit during the daylight, would illuminate even the darkest corners.

"Andres," she said, stunned by the surrounding beauty, "Its... Words fail me." She looked back at him, her eyes shining with happiness.

He looked around the three-section room. The left held a massive fireplace with furniture arranged around it and a chess table set before a large window. In the middle of the room sat a wide space with another fireplace and a set of windows flanked by a deep couch and two high-backed chairs. The last section, to their right, contained a massive desk with armchairs situated in front of it.

She looked for access to the second floor which was ringed with beautiful brass fencing. "How do you reach the top?"

Nodding to a doorway set into the wall on their left, he said, "There are stairs through that alcove. They lead to the second floor."

"Do you know how many there are?" she asked, walking to the nearest shelf and running her fingers reverently over the spines of the books housed there.

"I'm not sure, perhaps thirteen or fourteen thousand." He noticed the choked sound she made and grinned, he had been looking forward to showing Ria this section of his estate since they'd left London. Imagining her reaction hadn't even come close to the look on her face when she'd opened her eyes, and he felt a certain pride in being able to give her this.

"Would you like me to call a maid to show you to your rooms? I know you've had a long journey and would probably like to rest as the others are." He noted her wide-eyed stare and the slight step she took closer to the books and laughed, saying, "Or you could stay here and read. I have work to attend to," he said, waving his hand at the desk in the other corner, "but you are welcome in this room any time you desire to visit. Even if the doors are roped off." He winked at her, receiving a hearty laugh in return, and walked to his desk. Sitting, he picked up the first correspondence on the large stack of papers and pretended to read over it. A feeling of rightness settled over him as he sat there, watching her select a book and make herself comfortable in front of the fire. It was a feeling he hadn't known he'd been missing.

Andres and Ria fell back into the quiet companionship they hand known before she became his grandmother's companion. Since they had arrived, Lady Marie dedicated her time to resting and simpler pursuits while she had the opportunity. When guests appeared, her time would be spent among them, and she wanted to savor her personal space.

Ria became his near constant companion. She was there in the morning, reading in the soft light filtering through the windows. In the afternoons, she took tea with him, discussing current affairs and the contents of what she had found in the surrounding books. After dinner she would sit down with him and play a game of chess or two. He was improving, but she still dominated the game. Not once did he grow tired of seeing her, quite the opposite in fact, he looked forward to seeing her smiling face as soon as he rose and before he went to bed.

Sometimes his brother and friends would join them, other times he wouldn't see them for days. During the third week of November, his brother and friends had retired to the hunting lodge, wanting to enjoy their freedom while it was available. They returned several days prior as the first guests arrived.

Though they had to play host and hostess, amusing their guests, he and Ria still found time for a private conversation or game. Their time together had only cemented his resolve.

Throwing his quill on the blotter, he stood up and walked to the group situated around the fire at the other end of the room. Ria sat on the couch, her legs curled under her with a book nestled in her lap. Vince reclined in an armchair, watching Dimitri and Lucio play a game of piquet on a small table between them.

He took the armchair across from Vince, clearing his throat to gain their attention, and said, "I've come to a decision."

Setting a mark in the book she was reading, Ria looked up at him with interest. Lucio and Dimitri threw down their cards, giving him their attention, while Vince redirected his focus.

With the firelight flickering over his skin, throwing part of his face into the shadows, Andres reminded her of a dashing rake from a novel she had read. He'd done away with his overcoat after they had all retired to the library, relaxing in the comfort of their small group. The guests had taken an early night to prepare for the ball the next evening, which would open their event.

"And that would be?" Vince asked.

"I've decided Grandmother is right, it's time I take a wife," he replied.

Ria's heart stopped. Somehow, she kept a straight face and even tone, "Oh?"

She thought she had done a decent job of hiding the chaotic emotions hammering through her chest when she noticed the other three men staring at her. Vince's eyes flickered between his brother and her, concern etching his features.

"The most elite of the ton will gather here for the next month, what better time than this for me to find a suitable match?" he said, looking at his steepled fingers, deep in thought.

Ria swallowed past the lump that grew in her throat as she refused to show emotion that wasn't shared. Perhaps she had read too far into the subtle touches, the whispers, the way he looked at her. Trying hard to guard her heart, she knew a match between them would never happen, but at some point, he had crept under her defenses. She had no desire to see him with another woman, but instead, she sat there, staring at him with wide eyes.

"Of course," she said. It was all she could manage. She wished the other men would stop looking at her like she was a butterfly who'd just had its wings torn off.

Vince's jaw kept clenching and unclenching. His tone hard, he said, "Perhaps this is something you should talk about with Grandmother."

"I will," he said, waving a hand as if to brush the suggestion away, "but I would like your help Ria, you know the eligible women in attendance better than Grandmother does. You know me better than she does. I value your opinion."

"Of course," she repeated, standing, "I will go look over the list now." Her feet moved towards the door without conscious thought, and she closed it behind her. As the first sob racked through her chest, she covered her mouth to prevent the sound from escaping and made her way to her bedroom.

Andres watched her leave absently as he thought about his plans. If all went well, he would have a month to court the girl she helped him choose, and announce the betrothal at the last ball of the year.

"You're a bastard," Vince told him.

His head shot up to see each of the men glaring at him with anger, their postures rigid. Frowning back at them, he cocked his head to the side, "Why are you upset with me?"

Vince looked ready to jump from the chair but, suddenly, a smile split his face, and he said, "So this means Ria is available to court?"

"What?" his heart beat faster but he kept his face blank.

"I've been thinking of settling down as well. I think she would make an amazing wife and mother to my children. Don't worry, I'll still let her visit you, when she isn't gravid of course. Though that won't be often," Vince replied with a smug smile. Lucio and Dimitri watched them for a moment before merriment erupted on their own faces.

"No," Dimitri said, "I will marry her. She will be the figurehead of my fleet. I will take her to exotic locations, all the places she has read about or wishes to discover."

Lucio laughed, "As if a smelly ship is where such a beautiful woman belongs. I will take her home with me to ride bareback through the vineyards. She will be delighted with the Italian countryside, and I will make love to her under the stars."

Andres glared at each of them, growing more upset as he imagined them pawing at her soft, sweet flesh. The thought of her looking at them with love and passion nearly drove him insane.

"Regardless," Lucio continued, his face serious now, "such an amazing woman deserves a man who will love her. She deserves to be put on a pedestal, not a shelf. May the best man win." He grinned at his companions as they voiced their assent.

Chapter 11

Andres stood with Vince in the parlor outside of their grandmother's chambers. They waited in silence for the women to finish dressing so they could descend the grand staircase to formally open the ball. He would dance the first waltz with Ria, his grandmother declining due to a sore knee. The other couples would join them after they began dancing.

Two ladies' maids opened the doors to the bedchamber, drawing their attention. Ria entered the room first and took his breath away. Because she was in half mourning for her grandfather, she wore a deep purple silk dress with see-through black gauze covering it. The dark coloring of her dress accentuated her skin, lightening it to a soft ivory, and set her green eyes to a blazing radiance. Jet and amethyst stones adorned low cut trim of her dress. The stones also decorated the small braids holding her golden hair in place and hung from her ears.

He stared at her in awe; he knew he stared at her, but he couldn't help himself. Walking forward, he took her hand, placing it on his arm as Vince did the same for their Grandmother. He didn't notice the older woman's glare.

"You are a vision," he said to her, his voice soft with reverence. He searched her eyes seeing sadness that hadn't been there before. It differed from the sadness she'd shown since her grandfather's passing, and he didn't understand it.

She looked away from him and smiled, "Thank you. Shall we go down?" He nodded, gazing at her for a moment longer, and led their party to the grand staircase. The guests below hushed when they saw them start their descent, murmuring to one another behind fans. Keeping her head high, she held herself with more poise than the Duchess. He admired her.

They reached the ballroom, moving to the middle of the dance floor, and he turned her in a graceful motion. He placed his hand on her hip, striking the first pose for the waltz and the music started. As they moved, he realized she must have been practicing, as she was far better now than she had been during their last lesson.

She watched him while they danced, saying nothing to him. Her silence unnerved him.

"What are you thinking?" he asked her, examining her face. Others entered the floor around them, but they could have remained the only people in the room for all the attention he paid them.

"You shouldn't look at me like that," she replied, tilting her head slightly. He frowned at her as she continued, "It isn't proper."

"Since when has that mattered?" he said, his eyebrows drawing together as he made an indignant sound deep in his throat. She didn't answer him as the first set drew to a close and he led her off of the dancefloor.

Ria gave Andres a sideways glance as they walked together. The way he looked at her, the way he touched her, was at complete odds with his declaration that he wished her to help him find a wife.

She had spent a better part of the previous night with the Duchess, looking through the eligible girls in attendance, trying to decide which ones would be suitable matches. Lady Marie was upset with the whole affair, growling about what an ungrateful and stupid man he was. She agreed, but there wasn't anything she could do about it. Andres wasn't the type of man you poured your heart out too and crossed your fingers, hoping he would feel the same way. He was too stubborn for that.

Lady Marie had confided that she'd always thought Ria would be a good match for her grandson, they needed to make him see it. She'd laughed, taking comfort from the older woman, but ultimately believed it wouldn't work. They reviewed the guest list and realized there were few options available to Andres and, much to her regret, the best among them was Lady Kentwood.

She sighed lightly, releasing his hand once they reached the side of the room. The waltz had been something she had looked forward to for weeks, since they had learned the steps, but his announcement the previous night cast a shadow over the experience.

"You should request a dance with Lady Elizabeth Hargrove next. Her father is the Marquess of Lansdowne. She has a substantial dowry and the qualifications necessary to be a Duchess," she said in a monotone voice, leading him to the girl in question.

Lady Hargrove was young, Ria noticed, very young. She couldn't remember if the girl had her first season yet but knew, if she hadn't, it would be within the next year. Her family brought her to the winter event so if they hadn't presented her the season before, they would the next. Ria tried to keep ungrateful thoughts from crossing her mind, but she wondered if the girl had even hit puberty yet, her body being underdeveloped.

Andres grabbed her arm before she could approach the girl to make introductions, and said, "No, I refuse to court a girl straight from the nursery."

Ria regarded him, nodded and said, "Then your next choice is Miss Emily Ellis." She waved to a woman who appeared to be in her late teens. "She has no titles, but her father controls most of the trade routes from Europe to China. A match with her would increase your enterprise significantly."

She walked up to the girl and her mother, gesturing towards Andres, and said, "Miss Ellis, may I introduce, His Grace, the Duke of Northumberland." As soon as the words left her mouth, she turned and walked away. In her mind, she finished her part until the next dance.

"*Bella signora*," Lucio said, walk up behind her, "You are too fine to stand here and watch. You must allow me the pleasure of a dance." She laughed, closing her eyes and shaking her head at his foolishness.

"*Sì*," she replied, letting him lead her onto the dancefloor. Preoccupied with Lucio and the steps of the dance, she didn't see the dirty look Andres shot his friend.

Andres tapped the arm of his chair as he waited for the next course of the dinner. It was almost midnight, and they were only half done with the meal. Because he was one of the highest-ranking members of the gathering, he sat at the head of the table with his grandmother and brother.

His glance kept wandering to Ria at the other end of the table, sitting between Dimitri and Lucio. It seemed they had taken a fancy to her and didn't let her out of their sight. Even his brother had monopolized her time before the meal. The only time he'd been able to get close to her was when she introduced him to another young lady. He wanted to ask her what was wrong, he knew something was off. Now she was laughing and seemed to enjoy herself. Her behavior confused him.

After he'd rejected Lady Hargrove and danced with Miss Ellis, he'd met Lady Pemberton. Neither of the latter ladies had struck his fancy. The first, Miss Ellis, was deeply religious and had told him she was waiting for her father to agree to let her go to the convent so she could devote her life to God. He'd nodded and murmured in all the correct places but became convinced she would not make a good wife.

Lady Pemberton had been polite to a fault but distant. There was no spark between them, no interest, no life. He realized when he'd returned her to her companion she'd only danced with him to be polite. The way she'd looked at the other woman assured him she had no interest in him, if he married her, it would only be for convenience. She had said she was looking forward to retiring in the country and this was the last event her father would make her attend.

That left only one choice, one Ria told him grudgingly, though she tried to hide it. Lady Kentwood had the dowry, titles, and family connections to assure she would be a smart match. She sat next to him at the table, telling him how impressive she found his home and how she admired his lands. Agreeable enough in personality, though conversation was lacking the few times he'd spoken with her, one could not deny her magnetism.

He laughed at a joke she made though if asked to repeat it he wouldn't be able. His eyes kept drifting to the other side of the table.

As soon as dinner finished, Ria made an appearance in the drawing room with the other ladies, then made her escape. She was able to slip out of the room unnoticed, or at least no one tried to stop her as she left.

Walking down the hallway, away from the other partygoers, she heard a sound behind her. Intent on reaching her room and the novel she was currently reading, she was unaware of her surroundings. She realized she was alone in a dark and unused hallway that led to the family wing of the castle.

"Victoria," a voice said from behind her, and she closed her eyes, cursing her bad luck. It seemed she wasn't alone after all.

Turning, Ria groaned inwardly when she saw who followed her. "Lord Kentwood," she said, "To what do I owe the pleasure?"

"Don't act coy my dear, you received my message of course," he said, stalking towards her.

"I have no idea what you're talking about," she said with confusion, backing towards the side of the stairwell that led to their rooms.

He followed her, "I told you to meet me here as soon as you could get away."

"I never received any such message, and if I had, I would have asked for an escort to my rooms," she replied as her back hit the wall, the decorative paneling digging painfully into her back.

"Liar," he said, framing his hands on either side of her head and leaning towards her face, "I've seen the way you look at me, I know what you've been fantasizing about."

"No," Ria said firmly, trying to duck under his arm to escape.

"Don't worry, I won't tell Northumberland. We can keep this little affair between us," he said, grabbing her arm roughly to hold her in place.

"There won't be any affair between us. I have no interest in you. Go back to London and visit Lydia," she spat at him, trying to twist her arm out of his grip.

"So that's why you resist, you're jealous of your cousin's wife. Don't be, I've finished with her. The inane woman gets herself with child and tries to tell me it's mine? Wants me to challenge her fool husband to a duel and marry her? No, I'm done with that ridiculousness."

Ria couldn't hide her shock. Her eyes grew wide as her mouth fell open and she stuttered, "I don't know what to say to that. But my answer to you is still no."

"And I'm telling you that 'no' is not an acceptable answer. You should be so lucky that someone like me would be willing to bed you," he said. Using his free hand, he gripped her chin and tilted her head back, pressing his lips against hers while she struggled against him with renewed force.

Ria wanted to scream, but if she opened her mouth, she had no doubt he would take advantage. Clenching her jaw and pursing her lips against him, she tried harder to push him away. Suddenly, he was ripped off of her, stumbling away as another man stepped between them.

Looking up, Ria saw long light brown hair tied into a queue, and realized it was Lucio. Crying with relief, she grabbed the back of his coat and buried her face in it.

He didn't move as another voice she figured was Dimitri, said, "Stay away from her, she told you no."

"Don't tell me what to do cur! I am a Lord, and I will do as I please," Kentwood said. Ria peeked around Lucio and saw him standing at his full height; his nose turned up.

"Not where she is concerned. Of course, I would love to see you try to explain to His Grace why you've accosted his grandmother's companion in a dark and empty hall. And before you try to say she led you on, know he won't believe a word of it."

Kentwood growled in frustration, leaping at Dimitri with rage-filled eyes. Sidestepping, Dimitri raised his fist and punched Kentwood solidly in the jaw, knocking him to the floor.

"Pray we don't tell Andres about this," Lucio said, turning to wrap his arm around her shoulders. "I'll take you upstairs to your rooms, Bella."

When they were out of hearing range of Kentwood and Dimitri, Ria said, "Thank you for rescuing me. How did you know?"

"Dimitri has a long history of knowing when a shady person is up to something. When Kentwood left the game room, Dimitri pulled me aside with his suspicions, and we tracked Kentwood down. I'm sorry we didn't get there earlier."

They arrived at her door, and Lucio took her chin gently in his fingers, examining it for marks. "No more wandering through the house alone. Make sure there is always someone with you, one of us, the Duchess, or the staff. I don't trust that man to not try something again, even with the threat of Andres's wraith hanging over him."

He watched her for a moment with unreadable eyes, then turned, walking down the hallway. She watched after him, noting his pause before turning the corner to make sure she was in her room before he left. Entering her room, she locked the door behind her, before turning and pressing her back against it. Releasing a deep breath, she smiled to herself. Andres had truly amazing friends.

Chapter 12

ndres walked down the hall towards the library in a foul mood. After dinner, he'd been unable to find Ria among the guests. He had hunted for her, but she was nowhere to be seen. Eventually, he'd given up and spent the rest of the evening at the card tables with his friends. Dimitri and Lucio had excused themselves part way through the night then returned with no comment and stormy expressions.

That was five days ago. He'd seen neither hide nor hair of the vexing woman since. She hadn't been to the library that he'd known of, nor had she joined any of the joint activities he'd arranged for their guests.

He'd spoken to Kentwood the day before about his intentions towards Lady Abigale and his desire, on his grandmother's wishes, to keep the news private until the New Year's ball. It had taken less than a day for the rumor to spread through the halls. He should have known better.

From the other direction, towards the music room, he heard the soft sound of a piano being played. At first, he was going to ignore it, but there was something familiar about the playing. He followed the sound with curiosity until he stood in the darkened doorway of the room. Ria, dressed in a simple morning gown, sat with her back to him playing. He ground his teeth when he saw Lucio sitting next to her.

His friends and brother had, it seemed, found another pastime to keep them busy. They had also been absent from his side, an oddity since the four of them were inseparable when in residence together.

Ria played a chord progression and then looked at Lucio, smiling, and nodded to him. Lucio, playing lower on the keyboard, attempted the same chord progression with horrible results. He smiled helplessly at her, tucking his hair behind his ear, and brushing her arm with the back of his hand as he placed it back on the keyboard. Oddly, she didn't seem to notice.

Saying something to him that made him laugh, she reached over him to adjust his hands on the keys. Lucio's actions confused him because he knew Lucio played almost as well as she did.

It was when Lucio looked over his shoulder at him in the doorway and winked that he realized how the other man was playing her. He was about to step into the room and tear Lucio apart until he realized how such an action would embarrass her. Instead, he clenched his jaw and turned to go about his business.

Ria stood in the library, in front of one of the shelves, scanning the books it contained. She had successfully avoided Andres for over a week, trying to distance herself from him. Knowing she couldn't keep cowering away and that she would have to see him at some point, she'd needed time to come to terms with his engagement decision.

"Ria," a voice said behind her. She closed her eyes and sighed. Having double checked his schedule, Andres should currently be hunting with the other men.

"Good morning," she replied with a smile, turning towards him. "You aren't hunting?"

"I had other affairs to attend to," he said.

"Then I won't interrupt you." She moved to leave the room, but he stepped into her path.

"Play a game of chess with me, I need to clear my head."

She wavered, she wanted to deny him, but she missed spending time with him. Searching his face, she nodded and walked to the chess set under the window, taking the white side.

He took the other side, and they commenced. They stayed there until the sun waned in the sky and a servant came in to light the candles. He made her laugh, and for a time she forgot everything else that had been going on between them.

Towards the end of their current game, he looked up at her, his eyes sincere, and said, "I've missed you."

Her eyes flew up to meet his. She didn't know how to respond to that, but it turned out she didn't need to. As she opened her mouth, Lady Abigale came through the door to the library, interrupting their tranquility.

"There you are, I've been looking everywhere for you," Abigale said to him.

"Why?" he asked, frowning at her.

"I'd like to spend time with you, of course."

Before he could reply, Ria stood up smiling, "I think that's a great idea." Both Andres and Abigale frowned at her. She moved away from her seat waving to the board they'd been playing over. Few pieces remained in play, and neither had a clear advantage.

"In fact, why don't you take my spot? You only have two more moves until checkmate." She nodded at them and walked towards the door.

"Impossible," Andres said, studying the match. Though she left, she peeked back around the door and watched as Abigale picked a piece off the board, looking at it with distaste.

"This is such a useless, boring game," she said, "I can't believe anyone would enjoy playing it." She placed the piece she had picked up haphazardly onto the playing surface, and Andres glared at her. "My friends have a round of charades planned in the parlor, let's join them."

Ria didn't stay to hear his response.

At the end of the second week of their event, the household and guests woke up to a world which had been graced with Jack Frost's touch. Snow fell thick and heavy, covering the castle in a pearlescent blanket. Andres, hearing gleeful shouts from outside the window, peered through to see what was happening on the other side.

Children, some belonging to the servants and some brought with the guests, played on the white carpet. They built forts and threw missiles of packed snow at one another. Some of the older boys wrestled with one another as the girls watched, cheering for their favorites. Adults sat on benches lining the courtyard, watching the children play.

One person in the crowd stood out to him. Ria, dressed warmly in a dark wool dress and wrapped securely in the cloak he had gifted her, built a snowman with a few of the children. They had already completed the body and were working on the trimmings.

He watched as she lifted a little girl from the ground, holding her up to place a hat on the top of their creations head. When the girl finished the task, Ria swung her around, both laughing gleefully. She put the girl down, and a man walked up to her, ringing a brightly colored scarf around her neck, pulling her closer to himself. She pushed him playfully back, spinning away from him, and played with the tassels at the end of the fabric with gloved fingers. The man resembled his demeanor in such a way he could have sworn he was looking at a vision of the future rather than a scene happening on his lawn.

Ria, her face alight with humor, her cheeks rosy from the cold, took the scarf and wrapped it around the snowman's neck. A little boy ran up to her with two pieces of coal as if they were treasures, and the man hoisted him up, helping him place the objects where they had created eye sockets. When the man turned, he saw it was his brother, and a feeling of dark jealousy shot through his chest. Frowning, he realized he could be looking at the future, one where his brother and Ria played with their children in the snow.

He felt the rope that held their friendship together, which created their tight-knit family, was slowly unraveling. Standing in the dark and watching life unfold through the window, he didn't like path his thoughts were taking him down.

Several of the occupants of the castle had decided to leave for the day and enjoy the crisp winter air. Because of several days of frigid temperatures and snow, the lake below the castle had frozen sufficiently to allow for skating on the surface. The holsters saddled the Lord's horses and hooked several of the fancy carriage horses to sleighs to carry the Ladies down to the lake.

They left the castle with high spirits. Andres led the group on horseback with his friends and brother close behind. Ria followed in a sleigh further back, riding with his grandmother and a few of the older Ladies who had taken a shine to her. Abigale had also come, choosing to ride with her friends in the front-most sleigh. For a moment, he could pretend that everything was well in his life.

When they arrived at the frozen lake and disembarked from their transportation, Ria walked to the edge of the wonderland before her. The trees, frosted with snow and the ice, glistened in the sun. Taking time to admire the sight before her, she enjoyed watching the skilled maneuvers of the skaters as they enjoyed the majesty of the day, until she realized Andres was standing next to her. They stood side by side, neither wanting to break the comfortable silence between them.

Yelling rose from the group of young Ladies in their party, and they turned to watch drama unfold. Abigale was unhappy there were other people on the lake and demanded the footmen remove them so they could skate in peace. When she didn't receive the answer she expected, she started yelling at the top of her lungs, berating the poor man who could do nothing but stand there.

"Did I mention to you that Abigale is one of Lacey's best friends?" she asked, looking up at him.

"No, you didn't," Andres replied, watching the scene unfold with hard eyes. Abigale was wailing to Lord Kentwood who had also started berating the footman, demanding to speak with someone who could fulfill the wishes of his sister, the future Duchess.

Lady Marie stood with her friends, watching the commotion with a hard face. Vince, Lucio, and Dimitri kept looking between them and the commotion and sharing telling looks between one another.

Ria looked back towards the gathering, and said in a low voice, "This is your future. This is your problem to handle." He looked down at her, his eyes wide, but she didn't give him a second glance as she walked away to join the others who donned skates. Dimitri held out a pair for her, and she smiled, sitting on a seat the servants had set out, and letting him help her put them on.

Andres sighed as he went to settle the dispute. The day had gone from bright to gloomy in a matter of moments and had a feeling it wouldn't get any better.

Andres stood in the doorway of the library watching Ria look out the window. She hadn't noticed his presence yet, and for once she was alone. The others had been hounding her heels for weeks, never letting her alone. He was upset with them and intended to tell them as soon as he could get them into a room together. They had taken to leaving the room every time Abigale entered, refusing to be in the same space with her and their actions were noticed.

Ria had become impossible to locate during the day; their time spent together over the last months a fond memory that guided him through the darkness of his present. He walked up behind her, as he had done so many times in the past, and placed his hands on her hips. Immediately he noticed her bones were more defined. She had lost weight over the last month, and he became concerned.

Before he could ask her if she was feeling well, she stiffened and stepped out of his embrace. He caught the scent of lavender and mint, one he sorely missed, and resisted closing his eyes to savor the smell.

"What are you thinking about?" he asked instead.

She looked around the room, her eyes filled with sadness, and said, "How much I will miss this place, how it has come to feel like home in the short time I've been here."

"You're always welcome in my home, in my libraries. I've told you that," he said, his eyebrows drawing together in a frown.

She studied his face, her head tilting, and replied, "Will I be though?"

"Of course," he said, taking a step towards her, his face a mask of confusion. Taking an equal step back, she gave him a half smile, her eyes misting, and it broke his heart to see it.

"You'll marry soon," she said, "I don't believe your new wife will agree. I'll be going to Thornbridge when this event is over." She looked down at a spot in the center of his chest, "I feel I won't be returning to London."

"Ria," he said, tipping her chin up so he could see her eyes, running his thumb over her jawline.

She hesitated but turned her face from his grasp, looking down at her clasped hands. Her knuckles were white from the pressure of her grip as she started to turn away from him. He stopped her from turning with a hand on her elbow, wanting to comfort her but not knowing how to proceed. The doors opened behind him, and he turned to reprimand the offender for interrupting them until he saw it was Abigale. He stepped away from Ria, watching the stoic mask that fell over her face.

Abigale walked over to them, glaring at Ria, and sneered, "Shouldn't you be babysitting His Grace's grandmother? That's the only reason you're here isn't it?"

His temper flared. He couldn't believe she would talk to Ria in such a way. Before he could say anything, Ria simply nodded, "My Lady, Your Grace."

As she said the words, she looked into his eyes. He would have sworn if eyes could scream pain that's what he would have seen. He watched her walk away, leaving him with his future wife, and her emotion echoed in his soul.

Chapter 13

"Marry me, Ria. Be my wife. We could make each other deliriously happy."

Ria closed the book she held with a snap, glaring at Vince, "The answer was no the first time you asked, the answer was no the last time you asked, the answer is no now, and will be no the next time you ask." She tilted her head down, looking at him through the top of her eyelashes, "So stop asking."

Lucio laughed but seemed to be looking off into the distance over her shoulder. She shook her head and sighed, "The lot of you are too silly. I pity the women who have to put up with you for the rest of their lives."

"In all seriousness, why haven't you married, Ria?" Dimitri asked, his voice soft but curious.

She looked at the three of them. They had been good to her over the past few weeks. Keeping her entertained and warding off the creeping loneliness, they had also kept Kentwood from harassing her. It was Christmas Eve, and they had retired to their favorite spot in the library, hiding from the rest of the world.

"Who would want me?" she asked softly, after placing the book she was holding on the table between them.

"You joke and tease me, each of you proposing though my answer would still be no, even if you were serious," her laugh tinged with old regret.

Clearing her throat, she took a deep breath and continued, ignoring their shocked faces, "This world runs on money and power. I have neither."

"When I first came out, I had a small dowry, but my brother discovered the gaming hells, and he was never a good player. In fact, he was quite terrible. He came with us to London for my first Season and racked up enough debt to ensure he would go to debtors' prison if it wasn't paid off. My dowry was the only thing my parents had at hand to save him. So, now, I have no wealth to tempt a poor Lord with," she held her hands out, palm up in front of her, before folding them back in her lap. The men looked at one another in discomfort.

She smiled, as if telling them not to feel bad for her and continued, "My father was the youngest son of a Baron, and my mother was the youngest daughter of the Earl. I have no titles or land to tempt a rich man with."

"Last, I am no great beauty. I might have been able to do without the first two if I was. The only redeeming factor I have is intelligence, but to most people, that just makes me odd. That's why I'm not married," she said standing.

Turning to leave, she gasped when she saw Andres standing just behind the couch, between her and the door. She looked at the floor as she walked past him, not wanting to meet his eyes. He grabbed her arm, stopping her.

"Ria, you're beautiful, intelligent, and accomplished among other things. You would make any man a fitting wife."

She looked at the hand holding her arm, "You may think all of those things, but it's still not enough is it?" Breaking free from his grasp, she walked out of the room.

Andres watched her go. He wanted to run after her, to hold her and tell her that things would be all right, but he didn't even believe it himself. Turning back to the others, he came against three hostile faces. He'd never seen his friends so angry.

"How many times have you asked her to marry you?" he asked his brother, glaring in return.

"Several. She, however, is in love with a complete dullard who would rather choose greed over happiness," Vince said his eyes spitting fire.

"A man who has more land than he can oversee and more wealth than he could spend in several lifetimes," Lucio continued.

"A man who has the distinct privilege and ability to be able to marry for love but chooses to throw it away," Dimitri finished.

All three of them stood up, walking past him. Their demeanor enraged him. He wanted to yell at them, berate them for speaking to him in such a way.

Vince turned towards him from the doorway, the last one to leave, "You are always lecturing me on how our choices impact our lives and our family, brother. Heed your own words. You have a choice to make. One path will lead to happiness and the other to misery." He closed the door after him, leaving Andres alone in the room.

He clenched his hands into fists then relaxed them, repeating the motion several times. Walking over to the small bar in the room, he poured himself a considerable amount of brandy and shot the glass back, drinking it all at once. The alcohol would calm his agitation, he hoped.

The decanter sparkled in the candlelight, and he grabbed it, bringing it to one of the high-backed chairs in front of the room's center fireplace. After refilling his glass, he placed the decanter on a low table next to the chair. He removed his coat, cravat, and waistcoat until all he wore was his thin linen shirtsleeves.

Once he had reached a suitable level of dishevel for comfort, he sat in the chair and thought about his future. His brother and friends knew him better than anyone else, and he knew they had his best interests at heart.

Striking the first hour of the morning, the small clock on the mantel chimed, filling the silent room with a jarring sound. He'd drank most of the brandy over the last few hours while musing about his future and daydreaming about a certain little bookworm. He must have dozed in the chair. Picking up the glass, he tipped back the dregs and poured another. He was still uncertain of what to do, and he hated uncertainty. As a creature of logic and reason, he didn't know how to process the chaotic emotions swirling in his heart.

A slight nose startled him, and he realized it was the door opening. Perhaps if he ignored the person, they wouldn't see him there. He was in no mood to encounter anyone.

Ria walked past his chair, intent on the bookshelves on the other side of the fireplace. She must not have noticed him because she gave no indications she was aware of his presence. He wondered briefly if this was one way she had devised to avoid him. No one would expect someone to enter the library so odd an hour.

He said nothing as he watched her in the firelight. She was wearing a silk robe, and the view was all very domestic. His eyes widened as she unbelted the robe, shrugging it down her arms, and threw it onto the couch. All she wore under it was a sleeveless petticoat. A very short, immodestly short, silk petticoat that barely reached the middle of her thighs.

The small garment turned translucent in the firelight and left little to the imagination. He grew aroused as he admired her. Standing, he stalked towards her, his steps silent on the plush carpet.

"What are you doing here, Victoria?"

She screamed and turned, holding her hand over her chest. Her heart was pounding, almost causing her to hyperventilate. Andres stood over her, his dark eyes full of heat.

"What are you doing here?" she asked him back, emphasizing the word you.

"This is my home," he replied, taking another step towards her, "I can go anywhere I wish."

"I didn't know you were here, I'll leave you alone," she said, trying to step past him, head held high. His arm shot out, wrapping around her waist, stopping her.

"I don't want to be alone."

Her shoulders slumped in defeat, "What do you want from me?"

"I'm trying to figure that out myself," he laughed, though there was no humor in it. He drew her closer, studying her face. She couldn't help but stare back.

He brought his other hand to her cheek, gently pushing a curl behind her ear, "I've been watching you. Even when you laugh there is sadness just under the surface."

She looked away from him and swore she wouldn't cry as her eyes started to tear. He must have seen something in her eyes because the next moment, his hand wrapped firmly around the back of her head and his lips were on hers. How many times had she thought of this moment, dreamed of it? Imagination, it seemed, was no substitute for reality.

Resisting at first, she realized it was a useless effort. As she relaxed, he deepened the kiss, pulling her closer. He tasted of cherries and almond, the softness of his lips stirring a fluttering in her stomach that quickly morphed into heat. She placed her hands on his chest, moving them slowly up and around his shoulders. His muscles were firm and warm under her touch, flexing slightly as he moved the arm wrapped around her lower down her back, to cup her bottom.

Pushing her against the wall, he groaned, nipping at her lower lip. He took his time to explore her mouth, and she melted in his hands. Breaking the kiss, his lips moved to the sensitive area just under her ear. He played there until she moaned, his hand roaming down her leg and under her nightgown. She could feel his arousal through the thin fabric separating them. His hand moved around her thigh, his fingers seeking. His caress was as light as a feather.

Taking a shuddering breath, she tried to catch her thoughts, though they came sluggishly. Her body was on fire, she wanted him more than she could describe, but it wouldn't change anything. They would wake up in the morning, he would still be engaged to another woman, and she would still be suffering.

It took all her willpower, but she pushed him away from her. Confusion and passion warred on his face as he stumbled back.

"Why are you doing this to me?" she cried, her voice breaking. "Why must you torture me like this? You give me a taste of what life could be like, you hold me like I'm special and tell me I'm beautiful, but you discard me as easily as a scrap of paper." Inhaling, her throat caught and made a sound of anguish. "My heart can't take this any longer." Dashing past him, she grabbed her robe off the couch and clutched it before her, running for the door and the safety of her bedroom.

As she rounded the corner, she heard glass shattering against stone.

Ria reached the room she was quartered in without running into anyone else in the hallways. Her mind was reeling, and her chest hurt. Already having spent too much time pining away after a man she would never possess, she decided there was no way she could stay under the same roof with him, continue to watch him court another woman.

Pulling her travel chest from the closet, she threw open her wardrobe and examined the contents. Everything in it reminded her of Andres and his family. She didn't feel she deserved to take the things. Their agreement was her commitment through the end of the year, and she was breaking it. Shaking her head, she left everything but the cloak Andres had given her for her birthday. She was a realist, and it was cold outside, she would need it for her journey.

When Lydia had packed her things, Ria had insisted on keeping them, and they were transported to Alnwick along with her new clothes. She found the trunk containing the old gowns far back in the closet and pulled it out. There would be a mail coach in the morning that would take her into town. She could purchase a ticket on a stagecoach heading for Thornbridge, and she planned to be on it. Thankfully, Andres had let her keep the money she won off of his friends. It would be more than enough for the journey and accommodations.

Taking one last look around the room, she saw the portfolio sitting on her writing table. She ran her fingers over it and decided she would place it on his desk in the library before she left in the morning.

The clock in her room struck the second hour, and she realized it hadn't taken her as long as she'd assumed to get her things together. She laid down to rest before her journey started.

After Ria had run from the library, Andres had taken the brandy to his room and locked himself in. The next day he had no desire to speak with anyone and turned them all away, including his family and friends. When the snifter was empty, he called his valet to bring a full one and turned the worried man away, locking himself in again.

Perhaps he was being childish, but what she said to him had struck a chord. He had been treating her poorly, only thinking of himself and his comfort rather than her happiness. The way she looked at him had torn his heart apart though he admitted he deserved it.

The Christmas Ball had begun, but he didn't join in the festivities. Even when his grandmother came to rouse him from his lethargy, he refused to see her. He spent most of the night in a drunken stupor, not giving a damn what anyone thought. Eventually, his family and friends left him alone though his brother told him he was acting like a spoiled child.

The next morning Kentwood had come to his rooms, nearly knocking the door down, railing about his family and the embarrassment Andres was causing his sister by being absent. Andres had snapped, telling Kentwood off. He said he would never marry Kentwood's horrible, obnoxious, and ill-tempered sister.

Kentwood had then tried to placate him, which only made Andres more upset. Kentwood said the refusal would ruin Abigale. She would be the laughingstock of the ton. Andres had replied that they had agreed to keep the news of the engagement private. It wasn't his fault the word had spread, and frankly, he didn't care one bit what happened to the girl's reputation. She deserved whatever treatment she received.

Word he'd called off the announcement spread as rapidly as the original news. After breaking the engagement, he felt better than he had in weeks. He'd cleaned himself up and went to the library hoping to find Ria there.

It would take time, but he wanted to beg her forgiveness. He realized now the feelings of contentment and happiness he had with her could not be replicated with someone else. Thought it shouldn't have taken as long as it did, he'd admitted to himself that he loved her, she was the only woman he wanted in his life.

That was two days prior, no one had seen her, and he was growing worried. She hadn't been to any meals or events. Vince told him she had been absent from the Christmas Ball as well, once his brother finally started talking to him again. His friends had reappeared after the news of his broken engagement had circulated and acted as if the rift between them never happened. Kentwood and his sister had left for their home before the sun rose.

He shuffled the stack of papers that had grown on his desk during his absence, and he frowned when he saw a folder he didn't recognize. Pulling it from the stack, he opened it to see a stack of sheet music with a note on top.

Andres,

What do you give the man who has everything he desires? Something he can obtain nowhere else. To you, I gift a piece of my soul.

With all my love,
Victoria

With a shaking hand, he picked up the first sheet on the stack and looked at it. *Midnight Sonata* decorated the top, and he realized it was the song she played for him, the one that had drawn him to her. In silence he stared at it, hardly noticing when Vince entered the room.

"What's that?" Vince asked.

He looked up at his brother, "Find the Butler, ask him where Ria is." She'd once told him the servants knew everything, heard everything, no matter how quietly you whispered.

Vince frowned at him but did as he asked, leading the butler into the room shortly thereafter.

"Where is Miss Sutton," he asked the man.

"She left, Your Grace," the butler replied, wringing his hands nervously.

"When? Why didn't you inform me?"

"On Christmas morning, Your Grace. She'd said she had a family emergency, and she'd already informed you and the Duchess. She left with the morning mail coach."

He shot a wide-eyed, almost frantic look to Vince who turned to the butler and said, "Tell the grooms to prepare our horses and inform our valets we intend to travel lightly. We'll leave within the hour."

"You'll come with me?" he asked with relief.

"I wouldn't have spent so much time helping you realize you love her to let her slip away," he laughed in reply, "Of course I'm coming with you. I'm sure she went home, Thornbridge isn't that far from here. We'll find her."

Chapter 14

A ndres sat in the small dining area of an inn outside of Carlisle. He and Vince had arrived late in the evening the night before, pushing to beat the blizzard everyone expected would start within the next day. Their entire journey had been one setback after another and a journey that should have taken two days ended up taking twice that.

Vince had left earlier to secure a fresh horse for Andres' trip to Thornbridge. He walked through the door with a severe frown on his face, carrying a scrap of paper.

"What's wrong?" Andres asked Vince, sitting up. A servant brought dishes with eggs, several choices of meats, and bread to their table.

"Read this," Vince replied, handing him the paper and sitting down to serve himself from the dishes.

Andres's eyes widened before his brows snapped together. "Banns."

"It appears our dear Ria is being married off. The third posting was this previous Sunday. Do you think she knew?"

"No," Andres replied, clenching his jaw, "She never would have been able to hide this from all of us. No, I believe her family posted the banns thinking she would leave Alnwick on the first with the rest of the guests. She said something about her mother requesting that she return home for a visit after the event."

"Did you see the groom?" Vince asked, pointing with his fork.

Andres had to resist crumpling the paper, rage suffusing him, "Our dear Sir Garvey."

"Sunday is tomorrow, they've scheduled the wedding for the morning."

"Ria will not marry him," Andres sniffed.

"You're sure of that?"

"Absolutely," he said, standing. Throwing the paper on the table, he grabbed his cloak and top hat and headed for the door. Ria's father wouldn't refuse him.

"I'm sorry, but my hands are tied," Lord Sutton told Andres who growled in frustration as he spoke with the useless man. He asked the man to call off the wedding the next day and give him Ria's hand instead.

When he'd entered the house, the first thing he heard was Ria's piano playing. The sad melody tugged at his heart; he felt as if she already resigned herself to her fate. He had wanted to run into the parlor and comfort her but knew it would be better if he talked to her father first. The conversation was not going to his satisfaction.

"Please, explain again why you refuse to break off the engagement," he said to her father. He was standing in front of the man's desk with his arms folded, glaring down at him.

Lord Sutton picked up a slip of paper and handed it to him, then stood up and paced towards the fireplace. "My son, John, has somewhat of an issue regarding gambling. He doesn't know when to cut his losses. We haven't allowed him near any halls or tables for the past ten years."

"Ria mentioned something about her brother's issues," he murmured, not giving her father his full attention. His eyes widened when he saw the amount of the debt on the slip. It was short of one hundred pounds, not an insignificant sum but hardly one to worry about.

"There are about ten more of those still in Sir Garvey's possession," Lord Sutton said as Andres looked up at him in disbelief.

"What is his story?" he asked.

"I don't know why I'm telling you this," Lord Sutton grumbled, running a hand over his balding head. The man looked tired, and Andres felt bad for him. If Garvey had to blackmail him for his consent, it was likely he was no more thrilled about the arrangement than Ria would be.

Andres's eyes flicked towards the man then back down at the slip in his hand. There was something off about the ticket. He'd seen tickets from the small club called Gents before. It was a club frequented by travelers and the aristocrats who couldn't get memberships to Whites.

"Several months ago, John took a trip to visit a friend in Cambridge. Sir Garvey offered to accompany him. We hesitated at first, but John is a grown man, and Sir Garvey has known him since he was just a child. Somehow Sir

Garvey convinced John and his friend to take a week-long trip to London where they spent their time drinking and gambling."

"Go on," Andres said, holding the slip up to the fire. His brow furrowed. The slip was missing the marks William Gent crafted into the paper he issues his credits on. Making a show of placing the note back on the desk, as soon as Lord Sutton turned his back again, he lifted it and tucked it into his pocket.

"John swears he didn't take a loan, but after what happened last time we don't trust him. Garvey said he purchased all of John's debt and will hand the tickets over once he and Ria marry. If I refuse the wedding, he will call the debts and John will either go to debtor's prison, or the magistrate will send him to the colonies," Sutton said as he sat in a well-worn chair in front of the fire, his shoulders slumped in defeat.

Andres regarded him for several moments in silence, then said, "I will pay the debts."

"It's no use," Sutton replied, shaking his head, "Christian sent a note offering to pay the debts as soon as he heard, I assume from a friend in London, about them. Garvey refused. He said it's Ria or nothing."

Sighing, Andres realized he would get nowhere with the man. He'd already given up hope about his daughter's situation. Andres wouldn't let anyone send her brother off, he had too many connections to allow it to happen, but trying to convince her father of that would be useless.

"I'll take my leave then. I would like to speak with Victoria first, however," he told her father. The man waved him away, slumping back in the chair, and Andres shook his head. He would try to withhold judgment about her father until a future date when it didn't affect his life in such a considerable way.

Ria heard the door to the parlor shut behind her and sighed, burying her face in her hands. Her sister-in-law, Janey, had been in and out of the small room all day, bothering her about this inconsequential wedding detail or that. The poor girl was trying her hardest to make it a joyous affair, but no one was happy about the arrangement.

Her mother had been the first to greet her when she'd come home. It had taken no time at all for the delicate woman to break down in tears about how she had tried to prevent the wedding. She hated Sir Garvey and blamed him for what had happened to her. Garvey had always had a deplorable fascination with Ria.

"For the last time, Janey, I don't care what color bonnets the girls wear," she said, continuing to stare out the window instead of looking over her shoulder.

"Who's Janey?"

Ria whirled around in her chair and stared in dumbfounded shock at the man standing in front of the closed door. Andres reached behind him and locked it.

"What are you doing here?" she asked him, rising from the window seat, her eyebrows drawn together in a confused frown.

He walked over to her and took her face between his hands, caressing her cheeks with his thumbs. His eyes were soft as he studied her face, and said, "It took me far longer than it should have, but I've finally come to my senses. I know, now, that I could never be happy with anyone but you." His mouth turned up in a half smile, "So I came to beg you to give me a chance to repent."

Her eyes widened as he pressed his forehead against hers, "Marry me, Ria." Looking into his eyes, her lips parting as her breath hitched. He took advantage of her surprise, and his lips came down over hers, gently at first, then growing firmer with passion as his hands moved to the back of her head.

Giving herself to the kiss, Ria closed her eyes, wanting what she could have of him while she could. As his hands roamed down her body, pulling her into a firmer embrace, a tear rolled down her cheek.

Feeling the wetness, he pulled back with a frown, "What's this?"

"My father is making me marry tomorrow," she whispered, burying her face in his shoulder.

"I've heard," he said, running his chin over her hair, adjusting his hold to comfort her, "Would it be too forward of me to suggest you run away with me instead?"

Her head flew off his shoulder, and she examined his face. She always knew when he was bluffing. It was one reason she could beat him so often when they played games together. This time his face was serious.

"Really?"

"I'm not the type of person who comes to a decision and then gives up easily," he said, grinning at her, "I asked your father for your hand as a courtesy. Make no mistake; I don't intend to leave here without you."

"It's funny," she laughed, pressing her face into the center of his chest and enjoying his scent, "I always rolled my eyes at the silliness of the heroines in books running off to Scotland to get married. Who would have imagined I'd be contemplating it myself?"

"Don't just contemplate," he winked at her, "meet me where the lane and the estate's drive cross when the clock strikes one." She nodded, thinking of all the things she would have to do to be ready by that time. There was a list of things such as packing and hiding a bag, making sure her cloak was accessible to camouflage her in the snow, and trying her hardest to pretend she wasn't deliriously happy.

"Where will we go?" she asked him.

"I own land in Scotland, a keep called Cairnglen," he replied, "It's several hours north of the border but safer than trying to go somewhere such as Gretna. I don't plan on letting them find us until it's far too late."

"What about my brother and my family?" she grew worried.

"Do you trust me?" he asked her, running his fingers under her chin. She nodded, and he continued, "Then let me take care of it." She nodded and smiled.

"One more thing, mi alma," he said, angling her face up to his, "I love you."

Andres sat with Vince as the afternoon light waned into evening. He had just arrived back at the inn after leaving Ria with her assurances she would meet him later that night.

"So, you're absconding with her?" Vince laughed.

"It appears so."

"My upstanding brother, I never would have thought! Rent a heated carriage and cross your fingers the snow waits another day. Hopefully, the worst of the snow will come after you're married and not before. I would hate for you to be stranded with nothing to pass the time."

Andres shook his head at his brother. He was used to the teasing and though, during a usual instance he would tell Vince to stop. He needed him in a good mood. Instead, he took a swig of the ale the inn served as their specialty and ground his jaw.

"I ran into Garvey on the way down the drive," he mentioned, raising an eyebrow at his brother.

"This gets better and better," Vince chuckled. "What did the old codger do?"

"Tried to pull me aside and grill me about why I would be in the area."

"And?" Vince motioned for him to continue.

"And nothing," he sniffed in disdain, "I gave him a look and rode away."

"I'm sure he loved that. From little bits and pieces of information I've picked up, it seems no one around here likes him."

"Ria's family seems to feel the same way. Speaking of, I need you to do something for me," Andres said, pulling the ticket he had taken earlier from his pocket. "I need you to go back to London."

Vince didn't even try to hide his laughter, and said, "You can't be serious. It's freezing out there. We took almost four days to get here, it will take weeks to get back to London. No, I won't do it."

"I think these tickets are forgeries," he said, handing the paper to his brother. "Hold it up to the light. It's missing Gents signature paper defects."

"The handwriting seems feminine," Vince added, holding the paper up to the light and frowning. "Still, it's nothing you can't take care of yourself once you get back to London. I'm returning to Alnwick until it stops snowing."

"I don't want to wait. I'd rather have all the information at hand when we return rather than hunting it down myself," Andres replied. Vince crossed his arms and stared at him, his gaze unwavering.

"Cairnglen," he said, narrowing his eyes at his brother.

Vince stilled, his face going blank, and asked, "What about Cairnglen?"

"It's yours." Vince had been after Cairnglen since he was young, asking their father before his death to deed it to him since it wasn't part of the entail. Their father had refused, stating he was too young to run the lands himself, and they would discuss it when he was older. He had passed away before they reached a decision and Andres had kept it as part of his portfolio of land.

"Still," Vince replied, trying to keep a straight face. "London is a long way away, and it will be a lot of work to verify the legitimacy of those tickets. If they are real and weren't paid off, I will have to go about purchasing them."

Andres tapped his fingers on the arm of his chair, regarding him. "I'll petition Parliament for the Letters Patent to go with the land. You know I can. You'd be an Earl in your own right, The Earl of Cairnglen."

Vince was humming with energy but knew not to push Andres further, and said, "Deal. I'll leave first thing in the morning." They reached across the table and shook on it.

"I'm going up to the room to sleep before I leave tonight. I'll inform the overseers at Cairnglen of the change, and we will make it official when Ria and I return to London." His brother wished him good travels before they parted ways. Losing Cairnglen was a small price to pay for a future of happiness.

Ria's family, along with Sir Garvey, had gathered in the parlor for their last night together before the wedding in the morning. She'd had to act as if her life depended on the outcome of the evening, and when she thought about it, it did. Thinking over her options, she realized that even if she ran away with Andres, the marriage wasn't considered legal, and her reputation ruined, it would still be a better fate than being married to Sir Garvey.

Earlier in the evening, after dinner, they had retired to the parlor where Janey kept hinting that Ria and Sir Garvey should spend time alone to get to know each other. Sir Garvey had been questioning her all night about why Andres would have been there, and she tried her best to put him off. She pulled Janey aside and told her to stop. She didn't want to be alone with Sir

Garvey, knowing she wouldn't be able to avoid the lecher's grasp. The poor girl hadn't known what to do. She was too young, innocent, or both to understand the tension filling the room.

At ten in the evening, most of Ria's family stood to go to bed, and she followed them with glee. She couldn't wait to be out of the company of Garvey, who kept trying to paw at her until she'd wanted to throw up. He followed her around, making lewd jokes to her father and brother who hadn't said a word to stop him.

Sir Garvey had appeared moments after Andres left, fussing that her father should lock her away for the rest of the evening in case she tried to run away. Her father had convinced him she wouldn't. She cared too much for her family to do that. Knowing her brother's future rested on her cooperation would keep her at home for the marriage. Little did they know, she had every intention of running away. Now she had to make sure they wouldn't catch her in the act.

As everyone left the parlor, her father looked at her, his eyes sad, and said, "You'll be all right Ria?"

"I will, Papa," she replied, keeping her eyes downcast and letting her voice waver a little for effect. She didn't want her family to become wise to her plans. They still thought she would go through with the wedding to Sir Garvey in the morning. Her brother refused to meet her eyes as he walked past and her mother hugged her with tears in her eyes. Her father walked her to her room on the second floor, and she locked the door behind her.

Looking around the small room one last time, she sighed, her shoulders slumping with relief. The banked fire in the small fireplace in the corner still let off a small amount of light as she moved around the room, lighting candles. Luck was with her as her parents, and the guest rooms were on the other side of the house.

Moving to the armoire in the corner, she pulled the doors open and removed her cloak. The white of the fabric would help her blend in with the snow, at least she hoped it would. She took a spare dress, rolling it into a tight bundle and shoving it, along with a few underthings, into a spare pillowcase.

Considering the bed, she pulled spare pillows out of the armoire and placed them under the covers until they resembled a sleeping body. Studying her handiwork, she cringed, hoping no one would look too closely until it was too late.

There was a knock on her door, causing her to whip around in fright. When she remembered she locked it, she let out a long breath before answering, "Who is it?"

"Garvey, I would like to speak with you, please let me in," the man on the other side of the door said. Ria sniffed, there was no way she would open that door.

"It's not proper, Sir. Please leave," she responded, her voice hard.

He beat on the door again, but the portal and lock held, "Victoria, I demand you open this door right now."

"No, I will do no such thing, please leave."

"I saw Northumberland riding away from here today, and the bastard passed me like I was dirt under his nose. I know he's planning something and I want to know what it is, so open this God damn door this moment," his voice rose as he spoke until he was almost yelling," or I swear I will make your life miserable from tomorrow on." Of that, she had no doubts.

"I refuse. If you try to break your way through, I will ring for the servants and have you removed from this house." He didn't heed her warning, but rather pounded on the door harder, trying to break his way through.

She walked over to the door, rage suffusing her body at what this man was putting her through, and she screamed at the top of her lungs. Not knowing what possessed her, she vented all of her frustration from the past few weeks in that sound until there was nothing left. When she finished, there was no longer any pounding on the other side of the door, only silence.

Taking a deep breath, she tried to calm herself down, hoping the vile man had gone away. It seemed luck was not in her favor when he said through the door, "Tomorrow you will be my wife. I will teach you your place in this world, and you will learn to do as I say when I say it."

Glaring at the door, her jaw clenched, she didn't respond. To say anything would only provoke him and she needed him to go to bed so she could leave. She decided the bedroom door was out of the question.

Walking to the window, she lifted it and stuck her head out, looking at the area below her. It had been a long time since she'd climbed out the window, not since she'd been in the early blush of youth. She would leave this way, during the full moon, to sit by the lake shore and enjoy the sounds of the nighttime.

Since her bedroom overlooked the gardens, there was a covered trellis just under her window. She knew from long experience where she could place her feet so they wouldn't come crashing through the roof. Now all she had to do was wait, and hope Garvey didn't take up vigil under her window. She shuddered at the thought as she fell onto the bed, her nerves would too tightly to relax.

Garvey's attitude just confirmed her earlier thoughts she would rather attempt to run away to a life of happiness than stay and be a dutiful daughter. Her brother was an adult, and whatever issues he'd gotten himself into, he would have to get himself out of. Besides, she trusted Andres when he said he would take care of the matter.

Soon the clock struck a quarter past twelve, and she pushed herself off of the bed to blow out the candles, standing in the dark and listening for sounds of movement. When she heard none, she picked up her bundle and looked out the window to see if there was anyone about. Once she was sure that nothing stirred outside, she threw one leg over the windowsill and turned, drawing the other out as well before she lowered herself a few inches to the support beam of the trellis.

Pausing, her ears alert for the smallest sounds, she took a deep centering breath. Once she calmed, she reached up and retrieved her parcel from the sill before pulling the window shut from the outside. The cold air coming through the cracks in her room might alert one of the household to her missing status. As a bonus, having the door locked would lead them to believe she was sullen and protesting the union until someone could find the key or pick the lock.

Grinning, she moved to the side of the trellis, holding onto the long-seated vines. They were leafless this time of the year and made a great purchase for her hands. She threw the bundle over the edge. Muscle memory helped her to climb down the side without incident.

Taking the cloak, she wrapped it around her shoulders, lifting the hood over her head. She checked her surroundings before picking up her bundle and clutching it before her, her fists white from the nervous pressure. Running through the deep snow towards the tree line, her heart raced, and she felt as if someone would discover her at any moment.

Walking through the snow was tiring, but the exertion kept her warm. Just as she reached the front of the house, a light came on in the front parlor windows. Without thinking, she dropped into the snow, huddled behind a tree with her hood pulled close. She peered around, careful not to make any sudden movements while hoping she looked more like a snow-covered bush, and saw a large figure lit from behind in the window.

The minutes ticked by and she was glad she had given herself plenty of time to get to the lane. Her worst fear was that Andres would give up waiting and leave, thinking she wasn't coming. Deep down she knew this would be her only chance. If they caught her, Garvey would make sure she never left his home. After several more stressful moments, the figure moved away from the window, and she let out a deep sigh.

Gathering her courage but keeping hunched down just in case, she moved again. The moon in the sky was only a quarter full, and she was glad it wasn't brighter out. There was more than enough light reflected from the snow to show her the way, and the darkness made her a little more than a shadow moving through the night. She felt ridiculous.

The lane was a mile from the house and, at first, she had wanted to stay off the path the servants cleared earlier in the day. That soon became impossible due to the depth of the snow and the frigid wind blowing around her. As soon as the house was out of sight, she moved into the cleared path and ran the rest of the way.

If Andres weren't waiting for her, perhaps she would take a nap in the snow, and all of her troubles would be over. Laughing to herself, she knew she loved life too much to do something so drastic and thoughtless.

After what felt like forever, the lane came into view around the bend, and she could see a lamp through the trees. Andres was leaning against the side of the carriage like a devilish shadow in the night. When he saw her, he held open his arms, and she ran into them. He held her tightly as she caught her breath, rubbing his hands up and down her arms to warm her.

She noticed they had replaced the wheels on the carriage with skis, the wheels stored on the back of the vehicle. Andres opened the door to the carriage and helped her in, signaling to the driver their readiness. He climbed in behind her, grabbing blankets from the opposite bench, and wrapping them around her. There was a small heater in the middle of the carriage that held embers of coal, warming the small space against the freezing temperatures outside.

"I was almost scared you wouldn't come," he said to her, sitting by her side and gathering her into his arms.

"I wouldn't let you off that easily," she replied, grinning like a fool. She had made it to him, and she trusted that he wouldn't let anything happen to her.

"Sleep," he ran his fingers through her hair in a soothing motion. "We have hours of travel ahead of us." As they set off, snow fell behind them, covering their tracks.

Chapter 15

The trip to Cairnglen was long, exhausting, and cold. They had followed the path which led towards Gretna Green, but at the village before they detoured to the east. Andres had paid the innkeeper where they switched mounts and warmed up in the predawn hours to tell anyone who may come through that two travelers had gone on to Gretna to throw off the trail. The innkeeper who seemed smitten with their plight, agreed to the plan as they set off in the opposite direction as the world woke up around them.

Ria was thankful for the heat that came from the coals in the holder, without them the cold would have been too unbearable. The driver of the rented carriage had wanted to turn back at the village, but when Andres couldn't locate another rental willing to go their way, he did what it seemed the problem called for and paid the man an exorbitant amount of money to take them the rest of the way. She wasn't fond of solving issues using this method, but when he explained to her, it was this or horseback, she relented. Neither of them wanted to spend the next few hours trying not to freeze to death on horseback.

Now, almost sixteen hours and several changes of horses later, they were pulling up to the front of Cairnglen. It was a beautiful old castle which sat perched on top of a bluff overlooking a vast lake. Dappled snow covered the rocky slopes, leaving a majestic picture against the pastels of the evening sky behind it. The view was breathtaking.

Andres, behind her, watched her face with a smile as they came up the drive and over a sturdy bridge. They had sent a rider ahead from the last village to let the occupants know they were arriving. A young child ran from the gatehouse as their carriage passed through to alert the inhabitants of the manor they had arrived.

As soon as the carriage came rolling to a stop, someone stepped out from the shadows of the doorway and opened the door, lifting down the steps for them. Andres disembarked first, holding his hand out to Ria. She took it with a grateful smile, using his help to leave the carriage on stiff legs. Stretching, she winced as one of her calf muscles twinged, but took Andres's hand and entered the manor with him.

There was a loud squeal, and suddenly Andres's hand ripped from hers as two red bushy blurs tackled him, pushing him against the wall. He laughed, kissing each of what she realized were two small women, on the top of their heads.

"Ria, I'd like you to meet the twins, Maggie and Marin," he said, placing them both in headlocks and leading them over to her, "If I had sisters, these two would be it."

"You do have sisters!" one said in a smooth Scottish burr, punching him in the side. Andres shrugged, grinning, as the two women wiggled their way out of his grasp and curtsied to her.

"I'm pleased to meet you," she replied, smiling back at them.

"We almost couldn't believe it when we heard," the one Andres had indicated was Maggie said.

"Not one bit, Andres hasn't been here for years," the other, Marin, continued.

"Why have you come?" Maggie asked, putting one arm through Andres's and the other through hers, dragging them into a parlor off of the main room to sit in front of a crackling fire.

"For the pleasure of your company, of course," he said, taking a seat next to Ria.

The women looked at one another and rolled their eyes. Andres chuckled while she tried not to watch them with open mouth fascination. The two women were adorable. They were identical down to their red hair, large brown eyes, and freckles covering their noses. Ria thought she was short, but the twins only reached her jaw.

Practically bouncing in their seats, Andres said to them, "I'd have thought time would calm you two down."

One sniffed, "It seems time has helped you master your fears."

"You fear of commitment anyhow," the other one said, grinning.

"I still have time," he replied.

Ria glared at him, hitting him in the arm playfully, and said, "We did not travel over sixteen hours for you to back out now."

"I like her," twin one said.

"So do I," twin two said. She would need to learn how to tell them apart.

Andres chuckled, "Before we get any further, where is the priest?"

"Marin, I believe Lord Proper is eloping!" The twin Ria realized was Maggie laughed, glee masking her face.

"I knew it! I told you that's why he came to Cairnglen!" Marin replied.

"Ladies," Andres admonished, although there was no ire behind the words, "please."

They both glared at him for a moment until Marin stood to send for the priest. When she came back, he said, "While we wait, tell me how your father is doing."

The twins looked at one another, having a silent conversation with their eyes. After a moment, Maggie turned back towards Andres and said, "Father isn't doing well. He took sick earlier this year when the first snows fell and hasn't recovered yet."

"I'm sorry to hear," Andres replied, considering, "I will need to speak with him before I leave. Does your brother still help with his duties?"

Marin made a noise in her throat, glancing at Maggie yet again, before responding, "Father and Connor aren't on great terms at the moment, it would be best if you didn't mention him."

"What happened?" Andres asked, raising an eyebrow.

"That is a tale for another time. Since Father is ill, we won't be able to move him from the Lord's chambers. If we'd had more time to prepare, we might have been able."

Andres waved a hand as if telling them not to bother, and said, "At this point, all I want is a soft bed."

The twins burst out laughing, bumping their shoulders into one another, and Maggie said, "I'm sure you do." Andres groaned and narrowed his eyes at them, picking up Ria's hand and twining his fingers between hers while she watched the proceedings in amused silence.

"Vince and I used to spend our summers between Alnwick and Cairnglen when we were younger."

"How is that brother of yours, anyhow?" Maggie asked, her manner nonchalant.

"Still single," Andres winked at her.

Maggie's face flamed almost as bright as her hair, "As if I would care one whit about his marital status."

"Right. See what I deal with? This is why I never come here. I'd much rather vacation in Spain or Italy."

Maggie snorted, "Is there any country you don't own a piece of?"

"Come my return to London, Scotland," he said, his eyes holding a mischievous glint.

Both women's faces lost all merriment, Marin said, "What do you mean?"

"I've recently removed Cairnglen from my portfolio." Ria looked at him with as much confusion on her face as the twins held on theirs. "It's one of the issues I need to speak with your father about."

"But…" Maggie started.

"Our family," Marin continued.

Andres held up a hand, and replied, "I will make sure the new Lord of Cairnglen takes care of you and your family. He won't put you out." Ria narrowed her eyes. He was in too good of a mood at the news for her not to be suspicious. She tilted her head and was about to ask him what he was planning when the priest walked into the room.

"You called for me?" the elderly man asked. He was a portly but jovial looking fellow. All the hair that should have been growing on his bald head seemed to migrate down to his face. He didn't look like any of the priests, well-groomed with an air of propriety, that she was used to. Nonetheless, she couldn't help but instantly like him.

Andres stood, holding his hand out to her, and said to the man, "We would like to marry."

"This way then," the priest didn't even raise an eye at the request. Instead, he turned and walked back down the hallway he had appeared from.

Shrugging, Ria took Andres's outstretched hand and walked with him down the long stone corridor towards the manor's chapel. It was a small structure with a doorway to the inside and one to the outside. A large stained-glass window cast a colorful illumination over the pews, surprising her with its intricacy. Maggie and Marin joined them along with another man who sat next to Marin, cradling her hand in his. He was grinning at Andres like a fool as he leaned over to whisper something in Marin's ear. She noticed the gold wedding bands glinting on their clasped hands and realized the man must be her husband.

"I'm sorry this isn't the grand society wedding you deserve," Andres said to her while giving her hand a light squeeze, his voice low.

She shook her head, smiling, and replied, "No, but it's the small intimate wedding I wanted." He chuckled as he led her before the narrow marble altar. The priest stood before them, looking at those gathered.

"Just so you're aware, we should technically post Banns if you wish to marry in the chapel," the priest said. "Now I've covered myself, let's start, shall we?" There was a small snicker from the audience as Andres glared at the priest, receiving a droll look that made him laugh. Ria could tell true family surrounded him here, people he had grown up with, and who he'd never had to wear a mask around. She smiled at him, imagining the carefree boy he must have been.

"Do you have the rings?" the priest asked Andres, and she worried for a moment because rings were the furthest thing from her mind when she'd flown from her house, but he produced two bands with no issue. He handed them to the priest who laid them on the book he held before him and started the ceremony.

As the priest read from the prayer book, she couldn't help but steal a glance at Andres. He stood tall and proud without a hint of hesitation in his demeanor. Catching her looking at him, he smiled, his eyes crinkling at the creases. She smiled too, blushing, as she looked back at the priest. It had only been in her wildest imagination she would ever stand here with him, in this position.

Her nerves got the better of her when Andres repeated his vows after the priest, his eyes soft as they searched hers. She felt the blood rushing to her head, and she swore she wouldn't do something ridiculous, like cry or faint. Andres squeezed her hand, and she blinked a few times, realizing it was her turn to say the vows back to him.

"I Victoria Sutton take thee Andres..." her eyes grew wide as she realized she couldn't recall his last name. He had just said it when he'd said his vows, but she couldn't remember, even just moments later. It had never come up in conversation, even on the carriage ride here. She was too nervous to think if anyone, his grandmother or brother, had ever mentioned it.

A mask of horror fell over her face, and Andres laughed, realizing why she had stopped. It was one of her worst nightmares come true. She panicked, pulling away from him, her face and chest on fire as tears welled in her eyes threatening to spill. His face instantly went serious, and he grabbed her arm, pulling her into his chest and wrapping her in a tight embrace.

"It's ok love, everything's ok," he cooed at her as everyone else in the room went quiet.

On the verge of hyperventilating, Ria said, "I'm sorry, I'm so sorry."

"No," he said, nuzzling her hair, "don't say that. Everything is fine." He pulled back slightly, tipping her head up, and asked, "Do you want to marry me?"

She nodded.

"Do you love me?"

She nodded again, taking deep breaths.

"Then none of this matters. As long as we are together, everything is fine, yes?" She focused on him, his face taking full center in her vision. Her heart, beating in a rapid staccato, calmed.

She nodded again.

He gave her another moment to settle, then looked at the priest, and said, "Can we skip to the end?"

The priest shrugged, unconcerned, and handed him the rings. He placed one on Ria's ring finger and slipped the other on his own, not letting her go while he did so.

"Forasmuch as Andres St. Clair and Victoria Sutton have consented together in holy Wedlock, and have witnessed the same before God and this company, and thereto have given and pledged their troth either to other, and have declared the same by giving and receiving of a Ring, and by joining of hands; I pronounce that they be Man and Wife together, In the Name of the Father, and of the Son, and of the Holy Ghost. Amen," the priest finished, snapping the book closed. "I'll save you the time of going through the rest of the prayers. If anyone asks, we had a full ceremony. Mention the Banns being posted," he winked at them and left through a third door in the side of the chapel.

"Congratulations! We'll make sure the priest draws up the proper paperwork, and we'll all sign as witnesses," Maggie winked at Ria.

"Don't worry, Marin was a mess at her wedding," she laughed when Marin snorted. "Besides, you're family now. I'll show you where you'll be staying."

Andres closed the door behind them as Ria covered her face with her hands. "I can't believe I didn't know your last name."

"It's not something that comes up often," he smiled and shrugged, walking over to her, and pulling her into his embrace. She took a deep breath, let it out, and melted into his embrace. Placing her hands on his chest, she gasped when she saw the ring he had given her.

"This is the Duchess's ring, she never takes it off," she said, looking up at him.

"You're correct, it is the Duchess's ring, Duchess," he whispered in her ear. The way he called her Duchess turned the word into a lover's caress more than a title, and it sent shivers down her neck.

Cupping her face in one hand, he ran his lips over hers with tenderness. She moved her arms up to wrap around his shoulders as her lips parted. He took advantage and deepened the kiss, pulling her closer with his other hand, cupping her backside. After a moment of such treatment, he pulled away, smiling, "I have been looking forward to this for a very long time."

He reached up and pulled the pins out of her hair, the honey strands falling around her to mid-waist. Once he finished, he ran his fingers through it and drew her close once more. Nuzzling the area just below her ear, he reached behind her and unbuttoned her dress and petticoat, his fingers caressing the soft skin on her back.

As soon as he undid the buttons, he stepped back, pulling the items from her shoulders and letting them pool on the ground around her feet. For the moment he left her standing in her chemise and stockings.

Ria unhooked the buttons from his jacket and reached up to push it over his shoulders. He helped her remove the tight garment, letting it fall to the floor. As soon as it was off, she did the same to his waistcoat.

"Men wear so many layers," she said, laughing as she reached for his cravat and unknotted it, removing the fabric and tossing it on the ground as well.

"I agree," he said, sweeping her into his arms and carrying her to the bed. She squealed as he tossed her onto it, sitting on the side to remove his boots. Ria kicked off her slippers as he finished and he reached over, pinning her to the bed with his arms. She laughed and pulled on the fabric of his shirtsleeves, loosening them from the waistband of his pants. He lifted off her and helped by pulling the garment over his head, tossing it to the side.

As she ran hands over his bare arms, he flexed while reaching for the ties that held her chemise in place. She admired his masculine grace and the smattering of dark hair across his chest, running her fingers through to see how soft it was.

Growling, he pulled the fabric covering her legs, gliding his fingers over the smooth skin that was revealed. Ria let her head fall back, watching his face, as he explored her body.

"So soft," he said in a husky whisper. Bunching the fabric higher, he lifted her hips and pulled the chemise over her waist, pulling her upper body up to slip it over her head. He threw it over the side of the bed to join the other clothes.

Ria could feel his arousal through the fabric of his pants as he leaned over her and took one of her nipples between his lips, loving it with his tongue. She gasped in surprise as arrows of pleasure shot from where his lips touched the rosy peak down to her core. Taking a deep breath, she ran her fingers through his hair as he kissed his way to the other nipple and showed it the same attention.

Nuzzling and kissing his way down her stomach, he nibbled at a spot on the inside of her thigh, just over the lace of her stockings. He pulled on the ribbons that kept her stockings in place, removing the first one then the other, massaging her calves as he worked the sheer silk down her legs.

Relaxing under his ministrations, he surprised her when he suddenly stood from the bed. She shot him a quizzical look until he unbuttoned his pants. Pulling the offending piece of clothing off, he rejoined her in the bed, laying to her side.

Andres let his fingers wander down her ribs and over her hip as he leaned over and took her mouth again. His kisses soon delved deeper as his fingers reached the folds of her womanhood. As his fingers moved, slow at first, she moaned into his mouth and placed her hand on his arm. Warmth spread through her in a feeling she'd never experienced before.

When her arousal coated his fingers, he moved them in a more demanding motion. He gently inserted one into her core, hooking it forward and rubbing a spot just under his other fingers. Ria cried out, tightening her grip on his arm.

"That's it, Duchess, let go for me," he nuzzled her ear, nipping at the lobe. She felt the band of desire tightening inside of her and all she could do was lay there, letting the feelings wash over her. Thrusting her hips against his fingers, she searched for relief from the sensations pooling in her core.

Faster, his fingers moved against the automatic thrusting of her hips, expertly playing with her sensitive nub before slipping a second finger inside. His eyes filled with desire as he watched her face, changing the thrust of his fingers on the reactions she gave.

"Andres," she gasped, "I..."

"Yes," he said, twisting his fingers as the dam inside of her burst. Her thighs snapped together as she cried out, shaking, her toes curling as she shuddered. Removing his fingers, he let his hand trail up her side and gave her a moment to recover before kneeing her legs apart with his thigh.

He positioned himself over her, supporting his weight on arms he wrapped around her, caressing her face as he leaned down to kiss her. She could feel his manhood pressing against her opening, and she spread her legs a little further so he could have a better purchase. With one hand he caressed her as he gazed lovingly at her, pressing into her with slow tenderness.

"Duchess, you will be the death of me," he said, sinking further before pulling out slightly and repeating. "I'm trying to be gentle, but you make it impossible." Kissing the column of her neck, he stopped when he felt resistance. He placed his lips over hers as he pushed through in one final stroke, seating himself deep inside of her, swallowing her cry of pain as he breached her maidenhead.

Andres stayed there, giving her time to adjust to him, before moving. "You are amazing, my wife," he whispered to her while placing soft kisses down the column of her neck. She moaned softly, wrapping her legs more firmly around him, holding him close. The sensations she'd felt earlier started again, slowly at first, until she realized her hips moved with him. She ran her hands over his shoulders and dug her fingers into the hard muscle there.

Reaching for a sensation she craved feeling again, Andres placed his thumb over her nub, rubbing in counterpoint to his thrusts. Ria cried out, her muscles contracting as the pleasure he gave her thrust her over the edge again.

"Ria," he groaned, thrusting once more, staying deeply seated as his climax overcame him. His breath was labored as he gave her a contented smile and kissed her. She wrapped her arms and legs around him, holding him close, reveling in their joining.

Finally, he propped himself up on his arms and smiled at her. "Stay here for a moment," he said, unentangling himself from her embrace and standing from the bed. She watched as he walked to a small vanity and picked up a cloth, dipping it in the warm water from a pitcher sitting next to the fire. Letting the cloth cool, he came back over to her and used it to help her freshen up, tossing it aside when finished.

Andres climbed back into the bed and pulled the covers over them. Leaning against the headboard, he motioned for her to lie with him, and she moved to rest her head on his chest. He tightened his arm around her, playing with the wedding ring on her finger with his other hand.

"I never thought I could be as happy and content as I am at this exact moment," he said to her, kissing the top of her head.

"I love you, Andres," she said, looking up at him.

"And I you, Victoria St. Clair," he replied, squeezing her fingers.

Chapter 16

rash of warm weather in the third week of January helped to melt the snow, making travel possible. Andres smiled thinking back over the last few weeks. They had spent a delightful time getting to know one another in a more intimate fashion. On the rare times they emerged from their room, they would socialize with Maggie and Marin, playing games or going riding through the lowlands. The women became fast friends, Ria winning their hearts as she had his.

Andres, lying in bed with Ria snuggled in his arms, nuzzled the top of her head, and said, "The snow has almost melted. We need to go back to London soon."

"Already?" she groaned, looking up at him with a grin, "But we just got here. Let's stay another two years."

"I only wish life would allow us that freedom," he replied, tickling her ribs. She squealed and pushed his hand away trying to escape his grasp.

"We'll leave tomorrow and stop at Alnwick to collect our things on the way. I need to speak with Mr. MacAra before we leave," he continued, pinning her down to the bed and nuzzling her neck.

"Who did you give this place to?" She asked as she took a deep breath, enjoying the goosebumps his actions rose on her flesh.

"Vince. I don't want the girls to know though. He's been after this place since he was young and I want it to be a surprise. I feel his obsession is due to a little redhead you've recently become acquainted with," he said as he moved his hand up her side, cupping her breast and gently running his thumb over the soft peak. "But first, it looks like I have things to take care of right here." A sharp gasp rose from Ria as he took the sensitive bud into his mouth.

"So, you've emerged," Connor MacAra the senior said. "We had bets going on how long you'd keep that pretty wee wife of yours locked in that room."

Andres shrugged, grinning at the man, "She could have left any time she wanted to, she just didn't want to." His response elicited a bark of laughter from the older man which turned into a bout of coughing. Andres stood next to the bed Connor laid in, his arms folded in front of him as he watched a servant bring Connor a drink.

"This damn cough. I can't wait until the winter has ended. The warm air will do my lungs some good," Connor said as he put the tankard of water aside. He didn't look well, his face pale and sweaty in the firelight.

Andres sighed, rubbing the back of his neck, "I wanted to let you know I've traded Cairnglen away. As soon as I get back to London and the transfer goes through, you'll have a new Lord."

"The lasses mentioned something about that," Connor said, eyeing him. "Care to elaborate on who our new Lord will be?"

"I'll give you one good guess."

"Ah, that brother of yours?" Andres nodded in reply, and Connor laughed again, "Well, I shouldn't say I'm relieved. At least I know your brother will do well by my daughters."

Connor scooted himself towards the headboard of the bed, the servant coming over to lay several pillows behind him as he sat up. "Leave us," he told the young girl who obeyed with haste.

"I have an interesting bit of news for you, though I would like you to keep it between us," Connor said, motioning for Andres to take a seat in the chair next to him.

"Oh?" he replied, sitting where the man indicated.

"Some years ago, quite by chance, I stopped through a village about a half day's ride from here after a hunting trip. The blacksmith was in the pub, and we got to talking. He asked me how my daughter and son-in-law were getting along," he said, watching Andres's face. "This was before Marin and Duncan married, so I was quite confused. Upon seeing my confusion, he described one of the twins and a dark-haired boy, richly dressed. Said the boy paid him well enough he overlooked their age and performed the ceremony."

Andres's eyes widened, and he took several moments before he could say anything. "Vince and Maggie ran off? They married? Why didn't you ever tell me, or my father?" the questions rolled off his tongue, his mind reeling at the implications.

"You know your father. He and I were as close to friends as one could be with that man, but he would have ruined Maggie. He would have asked the church for an annulment not caring how it hurt any of them," Connor replied.

"Father never was one to consider other's feelings, was he?" Andres grunted, steepling his hands. Laughing, he continued, "It explains a lot of things though. Like why he's never taken a mistress or shown any real interest in the women who parade in front of him. Most people think he's a hard catch. Our friends just thought he wasn't interested in women. It turns out he was being faithful to his wife."

"You can't say anything to him or let him know you are aware. This is an issue those two need to figure out for themselves. Maggie is sore tired of waiting for him to get his act together and be a husband. I see it in her gaze when she watches Marin and Duncan."

"I wish he would have confided in me," Andres said, shaking his head, "I would have given him Cairnglen years ago."

"You know how your brother is, won't take anything handed to him. He has to feel like he's earned it. What did you trade it for if you don't mind my asking?"

"I made him go back to London to take care of a few things for me while I absconded with Ria," Andres replied, placing his hand on the arms of the chair to stand. "Don't worry. I won't say anything to him. I wanted to let you know to expect him within the next few months. Victoria and I are leaving tomorrow morning."

"Travel well, Your Grace," Connor nodded at him, "And bring your wife back to visit, she's all the twins talk about." Andres laughed as he left the other man's company to collect Ria and spend one last night with her in peace before they went back to Society. He shuddered to think how many people would still be at Alnwick with excuses they couldn't travel home yet.

Though the trip back to Alnwick from Cairnglen was shorter than their trip from her home to the manor, they took twice the time to travel it, stopping frequently and for longer than they had on the trip to Scotland. Neither of them were in a hurry to travel back to London, knowing the mess they would potentially have to deal with once they arrived.

"What happens if they don't recognize our marriage in England?" Ria asked, worrying as they came closer to their destination. The castle, framed in the distance against the afternoon sun, looked welcoming.

"Then I will get a special license from the Archbishop," Andres replied, reclining on the seat next to her and reading a paper he had picked up in the village they left a few hours prior. It was outdated but still held information on the major stories that had happened in London.

"But what..." she continued.

He folded the paper down and gave her a quelling look. She laughed, "Sorry, I forgot who I was talking to."

"I couldn't give a damn what anyone else thinks. Not that they will, but if Society decided to shun us as a scandal, just think of how much time we could spend together at home," he said, winking at her. Ria rolled her eyes and shook her head. They were almost to the gate now, footmen coming through the doors to greet them.

When the carriage stopped, a footman came to the door and opened it for them, letting down the steps. Andres disembarked and then held a hand out to her, helping her down. By the looks on the servants' faces, he could tell he'd made a good choice. All of his people loved her.

"Come, we should say hello to Grandmother," he said.

"She's still here? I would love to," Ria replied, beaming.

They made their way into the house and to the Grand Duchess's sitting room. Knocking, they entered at her beckoning, "Good afternoon, Grandmother. I'd like to introduce you to my wife."

"Oh, how wonderful!" Lady Marie cried, standing from the writing desk and giving them each a tight and loving hug. "Your friends told me you had gone after her. I had hoped you wouldn't be too late."

Ria's eyes widened, "Did you know what my parents had planned?"

"I had an idea something was brewing when your mother was so insistent you come home right after the event ended. I had wanted you to stay for a few weeks longer to rest before starting back to London," she replied, taking a seat in one of the deep armchairs.

Ria and Andres sat together on the small loveseat across from her, and she continued, "After all of our plotting, it seems everything has turned out well. I told you it would."

"I didn't plot," Ria said, her eyes growing wide. She looked at Andres, "I swear."

"I believe you," he said, grinning. "I find it amusing that you believe I was the only one she maneuvered."

"What do you mean?" Ria asked frowning.

"Who do you believe sent out the invitations to the ball we met at? It wasn't me. Your family's social status wasn't high enough to receive an invitation under normal circumstances. Also, who told you about the library at the townhouse?"

Ria blinked several times before her jaw clenched. She looked towards Lady Marie, and her eyes narrowed though they didn't hold any anger. "Your grandmother wrote to me about the library here at Alnwick. She said its only rival was the library at your townhouse and that I try to see it while I was there. I couldn't resist."

"She knew I would be in and out, attending to business during the ball," he said, grinning. Lady Marie looked pleasantly smug as Andres continued, "I wanted to find a way to keep you out of your house and away from those horrible women, but Grandmother was the one who suggested she could use help to plan this winter event. She made it seem like it was my idea to contract you from the beginning."

"What else?" Ria asked, laughing while she covered her face, rubbing her eyes.

"All the times during planning our trip where she was oddly absent, giving us time to spend alone without a chaperone? I know you believe you didn't need one, but it was highly improper and could have ruined you if anyone found out."

Lady Marie waved a hand, "I wouldn't have let those old harpies ruin her. Honestly, no one figured out my plotting, except for your grandfather. But then, he knew me too well."

"Grandmother, how much did your knee actually hurt at the opening ball?"

"It hurt," she said frowning at him, "I could barely walk on that leg the next day." He narrowed his eyes at her.

"The ice skating, building a snowman, teaching Lucio how to play the piano, those were all your ideas," Ria said, her eyes widening.

"Meant to drive me insane with jealousy, I'm sure," replied Andres, picking up her hand and folding her fingers together with her.

He grinned and continued, "And it worked too. I was in a foul mood for most of the party."

"That I remember," Ria laughed, giving his hand a light squeeze and tilting her head slightly, "Why did you pick Lady Kentwood anyhow?"

"Because I was an idiot who should have opened his eyes and saved himself months of pining," he replied, wrinkling his nose at her, both Ladies laughing.

Lady Marie winked and said, "I told you to have faith. I've never steered you wrong before."

Chapter 17

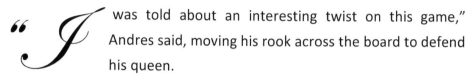

"*I* was told about an interesting twist on this game," Andres said, moving his rook across the board to defend his queen.

"Tell me about it," Ria replied, capturing his queen despite his best efforts.

They arrived in London several days prior, but his brother was the only person they had informed. Vince sent word he would stop by in the evening for dinner to update them on what he had uncovered. While they waited for him, they played a quick game of chess.

"For every piece you lose, you take off a piece of clothing," he gave her a toothy smile.

Ria raised an eyebrow, and said, "Why ever would you want to play those stakes with me? I'd be sitting here fully clothed, and you'd be naked." He frowned, glaring at her, and she laughed in reply.

"Have you heard anything from Vince?" she asked, waiting for him to make his move.

Sitting back in his chair, he tapped his fingers against the arm, considering her question. "No, Vince hasn't sent anything other than his intention to speak with us tonight. I have discovered that your father, brother, and Garvey are also here in London. They are staying with your cousin."

"But we figured they would come here as soon as they found me missing."

"It makes a confrontation more convenient, having them all in one place," he smiled, taking his next move and capturing her bishop.

Sniffing, Ria moved her queen into position. She had left the bishop open as a diversion, and it spoke to his frame of mind that he had gone for the play. "Checkmate," she said, looking up at him.

"Seriously?" he replied, studying the board.

"You're too distracted to play," she said shaking her head and standing.

"How do you play so well with everything that is going on?" he asked, standing as well and pulling her into his embrace.

She laughed, nuzzling his chest then resting her cheek over his heart, "Practice. You've only known them for a year. I've dealt with these people my whole life."

There was a knock on the door before it opened, admitting Vince and another gentleman. He grinned and winked at Ria as the two of them stepped apart, and said, "Your Graces, may I present Mr. William Gent. He is the proprietor of Gents Hall."

Andres nodded to the man and motioned for him and Vince to join them. Vince and Gent sat in the chairs nearest the fireplace while Andres and Ria sat together on the couch. They shared pleasantries for a few moments before Andres turned to Gent, "Did you have a chance to look at the ticket I sent with my brother?"

"I did," Gent replied, "and it's not one of mine. I can produce a sample if you would like. The forgery isn't even close."

"I'm assuming whoever wrote it didn't expect the ticket to make its way back to London," Vince said.

"And they would have been correct," Ria replied, "If it wasn't for my husband." She looked up at him, her eyes soft, and smiled. He smiled in return, taking her hand. Normally a couple with their position in society wouldn't show any affection to one another, but then again, normally marriages with their position weren't made on love matches.

Gent raised an eyebrow at her statement, and Vince offered, "The man Her Grace's father had planned to marry her off to didn't travel to London often. Her father and brother didn't either. There would have been no one to confirm the amount of the debt if my brother hadn't gone after her when he did."

"How much did they say the debt was?" Gent asked, curious.

"Around one thousand pounds," Andres replied. Ria made a dismayed noise in the back of her throat.

"And they think I would let a man leave London owing me that much?" Gent guwaffed. He shook his head and continued, "There is nothing I hate more than liars and cheats. Let me know if you would like any help with this matter."

"Interesting you should say that," Andres replied, "I would like to ask you to meet us tomorrow morning at the Earl of Amberley's townhouse."

Gent regarded him for a long moment before nodding, "What time?"

"Eleven in the morning."

Gent stood up to take his leave and bowed to them, "Your Graces." They watched him walk from the room, closing the door behind him.

Andres turned to Vince, "Were there any other debts?"

"A mere twenty pounds between a cloth maker and a toy shop. I paid off the tickets," he replied as Andres nodded at him.

"It's still so odd to me," Ria said with amusement, shaking her head.

"What is?" Vince asked her.

"Being called 'Your Grace.' I guess I don't get to live in obscurity anymore, do I?"

Andres shook his head, "And speaking of, Duchess, no more walks without a valet or footman. Not even to the corner market." He narrowed his eyes at her, bumping her side with his arm, as she blushed and shrugged.

"Hardly a month and you two already seem like an old married couple," Vince laughed.

"Not that you would know what that's like, brother," Andres replied, giving Vince a steady look. Vince cocked his head and examined his brother through narrowed eyes, but said nothing.

"Maggie and Marin send their love. It seems Connor has fallen ill, as the new Lord of Cairnglen you should go sooner than later," Andres grinned at his brother, breaking the tension between them.

"Speaking of, I've taken the liberty of having the title transfer drawn up. One set of documents for the property and the other set for Parliament."

Andres nodded as a servant came in to announce the evening meal. "We'll look over them after dinner."

Ria stared at the façade of the building before her. It was so familiar but seemed so alien at the same time. It was the first time she would be back since her grandfather's passing. Taking a deep breath, she steadied herself, wondering at what emotions would play through her as she walked through the halls of her once beloved home.

Most of her adult life was spent here, in the comfort of her grandparents' embrace, reading and dreaming about the man she would marry. Never in all of her wistful imaginings would she have thought it would be the man standing next to her. She looked up at Andres, studying the firm line of his jaw, admiring the confidence he exuded as he spoke with the magistrate and his brother.

Andres had tried to convince her to stay behind, they didn't want her to witness the conflict they were about to enter, but she would have none of it. She had argued that, as the one the conflict revolved around, she had the right to see it through to the end.

After hours of back and forth, with neither of them giving ground, she suggested they play a game, and the winner would decide. He'd thrown his arms in defeat and agreed she could come since it was hard enough to beat her without such motivation. She'd never had any intention of dropping the subject anyhow.

Gent arrived and, after he handed his horse off to a footman, the party ascended the stairs to the townhouse and rang the bell. When the butler opened the door, his face lit up.

"Miss Victoria, what a pleasant surprise," he said, holding the door open for their party, "But then I've heard it isn't Miss anymore is it? I'm glad to see everything worked out for you."

Ria blushed, "Thank you, Jenkins. We've come to call on my family, though I know it's early. We wanted to catch them before others called for the day."

"If you'll come this way and wait in the parlor, I will inform them of your arrival. Your cousin has been turning away all callers since your father arrived but I'm sure they will want to speak with you."

Ria grimaced as he led their party to the parlor. She had no doubts her family wanted to speak with her. Standing behind her, Andres wrapped his arm around her waist and squeezed gently, giving her reassurance through his presence.

Christian entered the parlor and, after glancing over his shoulder to see if anyone was behind him, turned to her with glee, "Congratulations Little Bird," he said, using the nickname he had called her when they were younger, before life took them down their current path. "I always knew you would be brave enough to follow your heart." For just a moment he was the boy she remembered growing up. There was a screech behind him as a very pregnant Lydia entered the room.

"What is she doing here?" she screamed. Christian closed his eyes and his jaw clenched before he turned towards his wife.

"I assume she came to speak with her family," he replied in an even yet frosty tone. She'd known her cousin was unhappy in his marriage, but being caught up in her own life, had never truly realized how miserable he was.

Before Lydia could get herself worked up, her family and Sir Garvey entered the room. Christian took Lydia's arm and led her to a couch, making her sit as she glared at all of them. Ria narrowed her eyes at the other woman.

"I'm disappointed in you Victoria, shirking your responsibilities and running off like a common doxy. You left your brother to the wolves with no concern for your family," her father said to her, his voice filled with anger.

Gasping in disbelief, she replied, "Then we can be disappointed together, trying to sell me off like chattel without even verifying the legitimacy of the claims against John." Andres tightened his grip around her waist, holding her firm when she would have taken a step towards her father while gesturing angrily towards her brother.

"And it is about said claims that we have come today," Andres took over while Ria glowered at her father.

"I told you I didn't gamble while I was here," John chimed in but quickly silenced when his father glared at him.

"I must confess," Andres continued, "I took the slip from your desk before I took my leave, but for all the best intentions. You see, I've had dealings with William Gent who owns Gents Hall, the gambling hall Garvey said your son frequented. Imagine my surprise when I took a look at the slip and failed to see the telltale signs of a legitimate note." Both Lydia and Garvey went as still as stone when he said these words.

Garvey, shaking off his surprise, said, "Impossible. I was there with your son, you know he's lied to you in the past. And now, you would take this man's word over mine? A man who kidnapped your daughter in the dead of night and forced her to run away with him?"

"You can hardly call it kidnapping," Ria sniffed, "I'm well into my majority, and I went quite willingly." She grinned at Andres, and he smiled back down at her.

"You don't need to believe me, Gent will be more than happy to verify my claims," Andres said.

"Go find the man then, and come back tomorrow," said Garvey. Ria's father looked utterly confused, and for a moment he almost pitied the other man, but he couldn't forgive his sacrificing his daughter to save his son.

"No need," Andres studied Garvey for a moment, curling his nose in distaste, "He's come with us today." Garvey's eyes took on a wild gleam as Gent stepped forward from the shadows. "We wouldn't want you to disappear before we had a chance to resolve this matter."

Andres pulled the slip Vince had returned to him from his pocket and handed it to Gent, "Is this one of yours?"

"No, it's missing my markings, and the handwriting is completely off," he said, holding the piece of paper to the fire while pulling a slip from his coat pocket for comparison.

"See here," he continued, " I also use a red seal on my notes while this one is black."

"Do you have any more of these in your possession?" Andres asked her father.

"No, but Garvey showed me the rest, they all look the same."

Andres nodded, looking behind Garvey towards the door. The Magistrate and the man he had brought with him stood there, blocking the exit.

"I believe the punishment for forgery and fraud is death, is it not?" Andres asked him with nonchalance.

"It is," the man replied, his arms folded in front of him, watching Garvey.

"She made me do it!" Garvey yelled in anger and frustration, pointing at Lydia.

Christian, stunned, looked at his wife, "What does he mean?"

"I have no idea what the brute is talking about," Lydia replied, crossing her arms over her chest, and looking away from them towards the wall.

"She said she wanted Victoria out of the house by any means necessary. I've been after her hand for years, but her father kept turning me down. Lydia said if I followed her directions, and claimed the slips were debts her brother racked up, Sutton would have no choice but to let me have her," Garvey raged, "If anyone found out, it would be too late to do anything about it. She would be my wife and no one would be able to contest it."

"Is that true, Lydia?" Christian asked her again.

"No, don't be ridiculous," she said, still not meeting their eyes. Christian shook his head, his face masked with anger.

"I believe she's one of the worst liars I've ever seen," Gent said, reading Lydia's expression, "and I happen to have quite a lot of experience in that area."

Lydia glared at him, her eyes flashing, but she spat at Ria, "I have no idea why everyone is so infatuated with you. You're a worthless nobody yet everyone bends over backward to fawn all over you. You couldn't even let me have Miles!"

Ria realized she must be speaking of Kentwood and cleared her throat, looking at Christian. He didn't seem surprised in the least to hear what his wife said.

"Perhaps if you were nicer to people, they would treat you with respect as well," Christian said to Lydia.

"What would you like us to do with them, Your Grace?" the Magistrate asked.

"Arrest Garvey. We will gather the evidence for his case. With any luck he won't be an issue again," Andres replied. Ria thought it was rather cold to send him off to the gallows, but she couldn't help remembering the way he treated her. She was much safer with him gone, having no doubts he would try to come after her.

"And her?"

"She's too far along," Christian stepped in, "If you take her now, the child may be stillborn, and it shouldn't suffer because of the decisions of its mother."

"What do you suggest?" Andres asked him while the magistrate and his partner subdued Garvey. It seemed he wasn't going to go quietly.

"Put her under house arrest. She will be confined to her rooms until the babe is born and then you can do with her what you will."

"You bastard!" Lydia yelled at him. His eyes held no warmth when he looked at her.

"Trust me, I'm done trying to be pleasant," he said to Andres. Andres looked down at Ria, and she nodded slightly. She didn't want her cousin to lose his child because of his hateful wife, and she wasn't going to be the one to tell him it wasn't his.

"So be it," Andres said to Christian, "Please keep us informed of her status."

He nodded and walked them out, whispering instructions to the butler along the way. Jenkins looked like he had been handed an early Christmas present and bonus all rolled into one. His eyes took on a sinister gleam she hadn't noticed before as he left them to take charge of Lydia. They could hear her screaming as she was led away to her rooms.

"I'm sorry for everything she has done to you," Christian said, taking Ria's hands in his. "I should have stood up to her, but I had no idea how spiteful she really was."

"You aren't at fault for the actions of others. I truly believe you didn't know what she was doing and would have stopped her if you had."

He nodded, releasing her, and held out his hand to Andres, who took it in a firm grasp, "We'll see you at the Season's opening ball at our estate, yes?"

"Of course," Christian stuttered, looking surprised.

"Lydia's not invited," Ria added, winking at him.

Christian laughed as they walked down the stairs towards their carriage, but she didn't turn around. She had no intention of looking back, only forward to the life ahead of her, with the man she loved by her side.

"Let's go home," Andres said, squeezing her hand tightly. Smiling at him in response as he helped her into the carriage, she knew their life together would be an amazing one.

Epilogue

Christian stood in the apothecary's backroom, looking out the window as he waited for his friend to bring him the results. He didn't see the traffic on the street but rather focused on his own thoughts. Lydia had been confined for the last several weeks, and she was trying to make life as unpleasant for everyone around her as she could.

Only the most hardened maids were allowed to enter her room, it having been stripped of anything that she could use to harm herself or the child she carried. The first day, they had removed all of her powders and scents, placing them in the room that had been used by her parents. He had sent them packing the same day she had been taken into custody. Lydia's entire family was the same, and he wondered how his father could have ever called hers a friend.

Two of the maids had come to him and admitted that they tested her perfumes. He honestly couldn't care less what they did with her things, but they seemed rather scared to come to him, so he humored them instead of sending them away. He had a long way to go before his staff would start treating him the way they had before Lydia entered his household.

They informed him that one of the bottles mixed in with the perfumes was odd. It was larger than most of the other bottles and half filled with a clear, odorless liquid. That declaration had stopped him, remembering something his friend had told him about an odorless, tasteless, clear poison.

"It's arsenic," his friend said, breaking him from his thoughts.

Christian took a moment to absorb the information, grinding his teeth. "What are the signs of arsenic poisoning again?"

"Acute poisoning will cause gastric issues, vomiting, abdominal pain, bloody diarrhea, among other things."

Blinking, he thought back to the issues his grandfather suffered from right before he passed away. He thought it odd that Lydia would be so attentive, serving Grandfather at dinner, pouring his wine at night. He had a horrible feeling this was the answer.

"Half the bottle is gone," his friend pointed out, "why do you think she kept the rest?"

"I have a feeling if the child is a boy, she intended to free herself from our matrimonial bonds," he replied, looking at the bottle in his friend's hand.

"What are you going to do?" his friend asked with concern.

"Replace the arsenic with water and pray the child is a girl," Christian laughed so hard he almost started crying, hysteria edging his tone. His darling wife had killed his grandfather and planned to kill him as well. The sooner the child was born, the sooner he could send her away to be locked inside of Amberley Hall and pray the ghost of his grandfather haunted her. Was the thought cold and cruel? Perhaps. Did he care any longer? Not one bit.

Made in the USA
Columbia, SC
05 February 2020